D1146052

Some other

Chitty Chitty Bang Bang

adventures from Macmillan Children's Books

Chitty Chitty Bang Bang
By Ian Fleming

Chitty Chitty Bang Bang Flies Again
By Frank Cottrell Boyce

Frank Cottrell Boyce

Chitty Chitty BANG BANG and the RACE AGAINST TIME

Illustrated by Joe Berger

MACMILLAN CHILDREN'S BOOKS

First published 2012 by Macmillan Children's Books
a division of Macmillan Publishers Limited
20 New Wharf Road, London N1 9RR
Basingstoke and Oxford
Associated companies throughout the world
www.panmacmillan.com

ISBN 978-0-230-75774-5

A CIP catalogue record for this book is available from
the British Library.

Printed and bound by CPI Group (UK) Ltd, Croydon CR0 4YY

For Mr Patrick Roose –
our very own El Dorado

1

Most cars are just cars. Four wheels. An engine. Some seats. They take you to work or to school. Then they bring you home again. The Tooting family car was not one of these. The Tooting family car was different. The Tooting family car was a beautiful, green, perfectly restored 1921 Paragon Panther, the only one ever built. Her wheels flashed in the sunshine. Her long, majestic bonnet gleamed. Her seats were as soft as silk and the instruments on her walnut dashboard sparkled like summer. The glossy ebony handle of her Chronojuster glowed invitingly. Most cars don't have a Chronojuster. It's a special handle that allows you to drive backwards and forwards in time. That's how special Chitty Chitty Bang Bang is – time travel is fitted as standard.

If an ordinary car breaks down it might end up in a lay-by with steam coming out of the engine. When the Tooting family car broke down, it ended up in an ancient steaming jungle being eyed up by a hungry dinosaur.

'Dinosaur!' yelled Little Harry. He seemed to think that the rest of his family might not have noticed the gigantic head swaying over the treetops, drooling spit and bellowing its hunger.

'Dinosaur!' yelled Little Harry again.

None of them had ever seen such a creature before. No living being has ever seen such a creature. But all of them – even Little Harry – knew what it was.

Tyrannosaurus rex.

'Hang on, everyone,' yelled Dad. 'Jem, watch the back. We're going to reverse.'

Dad pushed hard on the accelerator and yanked the gears around. Black smoke billowed from the exhaust. Sludge splattered into the air. Chitty Chitty Bang Bang moved. Six inches. Down into the mud.

Then her engine stopped.

'Why has the engine stopped?' asked Mum.

'It's just stalled,' said Dad.

No one said a word. They were all thinking the same thing. To start the engine, someone would have to get out of the car and turn the crank handle.

'If we just sit tight, maybe it won't see us and we'll be safe.'

'Or maybe it will see the car and think, Oh, tinned Tootings!' muttered Mum.

'Or maybe it will crush us underfoot,' said Lucy, 'burying us in mud so that over the years we turn into fossils and in millions of years we will be one of the great mysteries of science – a family of humans that somehow managed to get themselves fossilized in the age of dinosaurs. We'll be the Great Tooting Conundrum. Except they won't know our name was Tooting.'

The head loomed closer. It was so vast that Jem felt like he was staring at something through a microscope. He could see the bits of mud and twig caught in the folds of its pebbly skin; the stains of blood on its white, dagger teeth. Its tongue was as rough as a gravel path. Its nostrils were a pair of wet, grungy bin lids; its eye a tiny, twitchy rivet.

Maybe it won't see us, thought Jem.

But just as he thought that, those bin-lid nostrils twitched. They closed up. They opened again. The tyrannosaurus had sniffed, and its sniff was so powerful that every leaf and branch rattled and Lucy's hair went flying round her head. It was sniffing for food. It had definitely sniffed out the Tootings.

'Fascinating,' said Lucy. 'For years now there has been a debate about whether Tyrannosaurus was a true predator – able to move fast and catch and kill its prey – or whether it was just a very big scavenger, eating only animals that were already dead.'

'Why is that interesting?' said Jem.

'Because if it is a scavenger it will leave us alone, but if it is a predator it will kill us.'

'Actually, that *is* quite interesting.'

There was a sound like the sound that a house might make if someone picked it up and dropped it from a great height. It was the creature's foot,

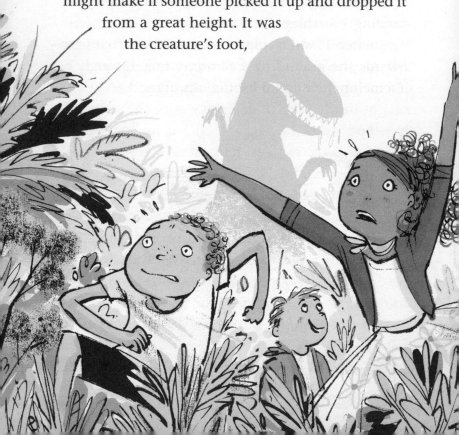

landing a few yards in front of them. Its curved, cruel claws dug into the earth as it steadied itself. Its toes stretched like leathery bridges. Its leg was a tower of meat. Under the skin, chains of muscle shifted like the gears of a terrible machine.

'On balance,' said Lucy, 'I'm going to say predator.'

Everyone leaped out of the car and into the undergrowth.

No one looked up.

No one looked back.

No one stopped running. Until they were all standing, breathless, inside what felt like a big green bus shelter. It was a single giant leaf, bent towards the ground by a raindrop the size of a melon. Jem found himself staring at the changing patterns on it surface. He could hear his father and mother discussing what to do, but for some reason he couldn't tear his attention away from those patterns.

'We need to get far away from that tyrannosaurus as quickly as possible,' said Dad. Not a sentence he'd ever expected to have to say.

'But what if there's another tyrannosaurus round the corner?' said Mum. 'What if there's a HERD of them?'

'Opinion is divided,' said Lucy, 'but it's definitely possible that they moved in herds.'

Suddenly Jem realized what the fascinating pattern on the surface of the raindrop was. 'Little Harry!' he gasped. For the pattern was the reflection of Little Harry's bottom as he crawled back into danger.

'Dinosaur!' giggled Little Harry – correctly – as he toddled through the undergrowth.

Without pausing to think, Jem ran after him. Surely he would catch him in no time. But it was amazing how quickly his little brother could move on his hands and knees. Unlike Jem, Little Harry did not have to push leaves and branches out of the way or clamber over roots and stones. He just kept shuffling forward, singing, 'Dino-saur. Dino-saur . . .' until he crawled out into the sunlight where the huge, savage, drooling creature was now examining the bonnet of the car with its nose.

'Dinosaur!' yelled Little Harry and waved at it merrily.

The dinosaur turned its mighty head towards him as Jem burst through the undergrowth and swept his little brother into his arms. He was about to turn and run back to safety when something stopped him. The eye. That tiny, dark eye was staring straight at Jem. The tyrannosaurus was looking at Jem, and Jem could not look away. Not even when that wide mouth opened, not even when that fence of cutlass teeth flashed in the sun, not even when that giant foot unhooked itself from the ground and swung into the air.

Then there came a terrible noise, an ear-splitting, tree-shaking noise, a noise that made Jem jump, a noise that went . . . Ga gooo ga!

Ga gooo ga? thought Jem. That's not a very dinosaury noise.

'Go gooo ga!'

'That sounds like . . .'

'Ga gooo ga!'

It was Chitty Chitty Bang Bang sounding her unbelievably loud original 1921 motor klaxon.

'Ga gooo ga!'

*

There was only one thing that the tyrannosaurus wanted to know about Chitty Chitty Bang Bang: namely, could you eat her? She put her mighty foot down and turned to look at the Thing That Went Ga Gooo Ga.

The standard Tyrannosaurus Test For Whether You Can Eat A Thing Or Not is: Does it try to run away? If it doesn't try to run away, it's probably not fresh. The Thing That Went Ga Gooo Ga didn't try to run away. On the other hand, it didn't smell off. It smelt sort of interesting. This tyrannosaurus was not a fussy eater. 'Interesting' was nearly as good as 'fresh' in her book. Another standard Tyrannosaurus Test For Whether You Can Eat A Thing Or Not is: Does it beg for mercy? Does it scream, 'Please don't eat me!' or 'Run, children, run!'? The Thing That Went Ga Gooo Ga hadn't said a word until now, but here it was saying 'Ga gooo ga!' This did not sound like a plea for mercy. It sounded more like a warning or even – but this was impossible – a *threat*? No one had ever threatened the tyrannosaurus before. She wasn't sure what she felt about it. It gave her an unusual feeling in her tummy. It might well have been the beginning of a laugh, but because she'd never laughed she didn't recognize it.

So she was already slightly uneasy when the next thing happened.

The Thing That Went Ga Gooo Ga threw a bolt of lightning at her. Every shadow in the glade shifted as though the whole forest was whirling. It felt like the sun had come up and gone down again in an instant. What was it?

Chitty Chitty Bang Bang had switched her headlights on full beam and switched them off again. The tyrannosaurus had never seen light so sudden or so bright come from anywhere and definitely not from food.

That was it. She decided to give up on the whole idea of eating Chitty Chitty Bang Bang and concentrate instead on eating those little creatures that were running around. Namely, the Tooting family.

By now Mum was happily hugging Little Harry in the safety of the bus-shelter leaf.

'How could you do such a thing?' she sighed, covering him with kisses. 'Don't ever run away again.'

'We have to stick together,' said Dad. 'Oh!'

Dad said 'Oh' because the melon-sized raindrop had finally fallen off the end of the bus-shelter leaf and exploded around his feet like a water bomb. Without the water to hold it down, the leaf sprang back into place on its branch.

'Amazing,' gasped Lucy. With the leaf gone, they could see the whole forest rising around them. Wisps of mist drifted between the tree trunks. A dragonfly the size of a bicycle flitted among the ferns, its million-colour wings whirring in and out of visibility. Beyond all that, the huge, oily back of the tyrannosaurus moved away.

'Now that,' said Lucy, 'is a predator.' She took out her phone – which was shaped like a big jelly baby – and began to film.

She was right about this. Tyrannosaurus rex was

a predator and like all predators it noticed every single little thing. This tyrannosaur, for instance, even noticed the tiny flash of light that sparked from the tiny lens of the camera of Lucy's phone. It turned its head around to get a better look.

The moment it saw the Tooting family, the tyrannosaurus felt more relaxed. They were definitely food. They were doing all the things that food was supposed to do – running around in a confused way and screaming their heads off. The screams in particular really got the tyrannosaurus's juices going. She swung around. She would be over them in a single stride.

'Run!' yelled Dad.

'But keep together!' yelled Mum.

'Hold hands!' yelled Dad.

They held hands and ran into the undergrowth, hoping that the ferns would hide them. The ferns didn't hide them. In fact their every move made the fern tops shake in a way that said 'Dinner's here'. The tyrannosaurus carefully lined herself up with the Tooting family's escape route. Her colossal tail swept through the glade as she steadied herself.

The Tootings followed Dad between the thick stalks of the primeval fern. With Little Harry perched on his shoulders, Dad dodged left and then right. He thought that maybe if the tyrannosaurus was watching them, this would make her dizzy or confuse her tiny brain.

Sadly he was wrong. All the dodging just made the food look fresher and more tasty.

It also made Jem anxious. He was thinking, What if we get lost? It was Chitty that brought us here. Only Chitty can take us back. If we lose track of where she is, we'll be stuck here, dodging hungry tyrannosaurs for the rest of our lives.

Then Jem stopped running.

And so did Mum.

And so did Dad.

And so did Lucy.

They stopped dead in their tracks.

They stared in horror into the undergrowth.

Something was coming towards them. Scything through the leaves and stalks and branches at amazing speed.

It wasn't the tyrannosaurus.

It was too fast, too low, and much, much too unstoppable.

'Duck!' yelled Dad.

They threw themselves on to the ground just in time as the something crashed out of the undergrowth and hurtled through the air above their heads.

It smacked into the ground behind them.

'Ga gooo ga!'

It was Chitty Chitty Bang Bang. When the tyrannosaurus swung around, she had swiped the car with her tail and sent her spinning through the air, right into the path of the Tootings.

'Well, at least that got her out of the mud,' said Dad. 'Thanks, tyrannosaurus.'

The tyrannosaurus probably heard him say this, because by now she was towering directly over the Tootings, with her mouth wide open, ready to swallow them.

Then she saw that thing. That Thing That Went Ga Gooo Ga went 'Ga gooo ga' again. Then it did its lightning again. Then the food that she was about to eat climbed inside it. This really worried the tyrannosaurus. To a tyrannosaurus, if food – for instance a family – climbs inside something, that means that the something has eaten the food. The something was eating her food, right in front of her. How unbelievably cheeky! The tyrannosaurus decided to think this over and possibly discuss it with some other tyrannosauruses.

The Tooting family settled down happily into the lovely soft leather of Chitty Chitty Bang Bang's seats and breathed deep, contented sighs.

'In all my long life,' said Mum, 'I have never seen anything so relaxing and reassuring as the sight of a tyrannosaurus walking in the opposite direction from me and my family.'

'Let's see if we can get this Chronojuster to take us home,' said Dad.

'What?' said Mum. 'We've come all the way to the Cretaceous period, we've just escaped an attack by a Tyrannosaurus rex and you want to go HOME? Surely we're going to take a look around first?'

'Take a look around?' said Dad. 'I honestly think from a health and safety point of view that the idea of taking a look around a fetid swamp full of flesh-eating monsters—'

'Not in a swamp full of monsters,' said Mum. 'In a luxurious flying car.'

'Oh,' said Dad.

Jem cranked the handle. Chitty's engine purred. Her wheels sliced through the soft ground and, when she was going just fast enough, Dad pulled the ebony flight button and Chitty flicked out her wide, elegant wings. They caught the breeze and soon the car was soaring up through the shreds of mist, slaloming through the giant conifers. When

Chitty's undercarriage brushed the tops of the tree ferns, dozens of giant dragonflies came skittering out, their wings a hurry of rainbows. A butterfly floated by – so big they could see the feathers on its antennae. From the top branches of a gigantic magnolia a family of what looked like stripy mice watched them intently.

'Strange to think,' said Lucy, 'that we're related. They must be like our second cousins nine million times removed.'

She took a photo for the family album.

Then all of a sudden they were above the treetops.

'Look at those weird branches sticking out of the treetops,' said Jem. 'They look like gargoyles.'

The moment he said this, the gargoyle-branches leaned forward and flopped into the air, opening up their leathery wings and stretching out their leathery necks.

'Pterodactyls,' said Lucy, taking out her jelly-baby camera again. 'They seem to be interested in us, and the feeling is mutual.'

Jem dug out Chitty's manual and started to flick

through the pages frantically to see if she had any form of on-board anti-pterodactyl defences. But when he looked up he saw that the creatures were surprisingly small and unthreatening. They were following the beautiful car through the clear blue sky, the way children at home might follow it along the pavement. Even pterodactyls could appreciate the loveliness of Chitty Chitty Bang Bang.

'Do you think they like chocolate?' said Mum, pulling out a bag of chocolates that she'd bought in a garage in Basildon. She threw one to the nearest pterodactyl. It folded its wings, caught it and threw back its neck to swallow it.

'The word today,' said Dad, 'is surely *unbelievable photo opportunity*.'

'Oh. Yes,' said Lucy. 'Do it again. I didn't catch it.'

They flew over the forest, tossing chocolate to pterodactyls without a care in the world. Until Lucy asked if she could have one.

'Do you think they'll be all right?' said Dad. 'You don't think time travel might have affected them?'

'Of course they're all right,' said Mum. 'Their sell-by date is a hundred and twenty-five million years in the future. Youngest first . . .'

She held the packet out to Little Harry.

That was the first time anyone noticed.

Little Harry wasn't there.

2

Most scientists agree that Tyrannosaurus rex liked to hunt alone, like tigers. But most scientists are wrong. Tyrannosaurus rex liked to hunt in packs, like wolves. There was nothing a tyrannosaurus liked better than running around in a tyrannosaurus gang, knocking trees over, frightening smaller dinosaurs. The tyrannosaurus's idea of a really great night was settling down with a dozen or so tyrannosaurus friends around the body of a large herbivore, ripping it to shreds while discussing favourite tyrannosaur subjects. For instance:

'Mammals – will they ever catch on?'

'Feathers – are they just a passing fad?'

'Comets – reality or myth?'

'Extinction – it'll never happen,' etc.

So when Chitty Chitty Bang Bang scared her,

the first thing the tyrannosaurus did was hurry off to talk things over with the rest of her pack. When she told them she had seen something that looked like food but which flashed light and made warning noises, some of them were intrigued – maybe this was a comet? Maybe it was the End of the World? Others just said she was a fussy eater. But all of them wanted to know more. The whole pack trooped back to the glade where the tyrannosaurus had had her strange encounter.

The ground shook. Trees crashed. Everything in their path that could run ran. Thirteen fully grown tyrannosauruses thrashed through the forest to the very spot where Little Harry was waiting.

The moment before Chitty took off on her flight across the treetops, Little Harry had slipped out of his seat and clambered over the door. He had waited all his life to see real dinosaurs and he couldn't understand why his family wanted to get away from them. When the whole mud-churning, tree-barging, tail-thrashing, cutlass-toothed pack of tyrannosaurs burst roaring back into the glade, Little Harry clapped his hands and cheered, as though Santa and his reindeer had just dropped in to offer him his own personal Christmas.

The tyrannosaurs on the other hand were disappointed. They'd come to see flashing lights and hear terrifying klaxons, not just another obviously-edible-but-not-very-meaty mammal. 'Oh well,' thought thirteen tyrannosaurs at the same time, 'at least I get a snack out of it.' And thirteen tyrannosaur heads bent down to swallow Little Harry.

The thing that saved him was that – unlike any other creature that has ever lived – he ran *towards* the tyrannosaurs. No one runs *towards* a hungry tyrannosaur. Even baby tyrannosaurs do no run towards Mummy when Mummy is hungry, because – horrible but true – family loyalty means very little when a tyrannosaurus is hungry.

Little Harry, however, ran forward. He ran right under the tyrannosauruses' heads, hoping to get a better view of their funny little arms. Tyrannosaurs have many talents but backing up is not one of them. When Little Harry ran out of reach of their mouths, some of them tried to turn to the right, some tried to turn to the left, some tried to go right round, some just stood there, bewildered. The result was a lot of tyrannosaurs banging heads. And the result of that was a lot of angry tyrannosaurs. Little Harry loved this more than anything. As giant killer lizards bit huge bloody chunks out of each other and clawed and bellowed in pain and fury, Little Harry clapped his hands and yelled, 'Again!'

This behaviour did slightly refocus the tyrannosaurs' attention on Little Harry. The cleverer ones managed to get themselves into a good position to snatch him up in their jaws. But just then . . .

'Ga gooo ga!'

Chitty Chitty Bang Bang flew back into the clearing. Lights flashing. Klaxon sounding. No one had mentioned before that the mysterious object could fly. The only thing they'd ever heard of that could fly and flash light at the same time was a comet. And all they knew about comets was that they made you extinct. With all the grace and precision of a troupe of seven-ton ballerinas, the tyrannosaurs spun on their three-toed feet and fled from the scene.

'Dinosaurs!' yelled Little Harry, as his mother swept him into her arms.

'Yes,' she said, 'we noticed them.'

'Let's get out of here and go home.' Dad grabbed the handle of the Chronojuster.

'Whoa!' said Jem. 'Not so fast! We don't want to end up in some distant future where the whole world is flooded and everyone's got gills.'

'Good thinking, Jem,' said Dad. 'That was a narrow escape. Gently does it.'

'Although,' said Lucy, 'a post-apocalyptic

submarine future does sound quite interesting.'

'Not as interesting as getting safely back to Basildon,' said Dad, moving the lever gently forward.

The Tootings' first time-trip had been so sudden and unexpected they hadn't really noticed what it felt like. This time, though, as the giant ferns around them trembled, blurred and then vanished, they were able to enjoy the strange tingly sensation that time travel gives you. It's like a cool breeze that seems to pass straight through your body, filtering through all your cells. A wide, red desert unrolled beneath them like a carpet. The sky filled up with unexpected colours and towers of red and purple cloud. Lightning flickered, illuminating great piles of bleached bones.

'I think we just passed through the mass extinction at the end of the Cretaceous,' said Lucy.

'So nearly Basildon then?' said Dad.

'Just another sixty-six million years,' said Lucy. 'Oh!'

Everyone said 'Oh!' at the same time, because all across the sky, the menacing clouds turned white and fluffy and the dark sky turned bright blue. Blades of tall grass popped up from the sand like quick green fireworks until the whole desert became a rippling savannah where the long necks of big birds rose up like feathery periscopes. Then, as if an invisible hand were wiping the whole landscape clean with a cloth, a strange blankness began to spread from east to west. The land was turning white, the sky grey.

'The Ice Age is coming,' said Jem. 'Do we have any antifreeze?'

'I'm not sure,' said Dad. 'Maybe the best thing is to speed up.'

So the whole Ice Age rolled over them quick as a spring shower, leaving just a caster-sugar dusting of frost on the bonnet. As soon as the glaciers had gone by, Dad slowed down again so that they could watch the mighty new rivers pouring over the land. A brown bubbling torrent ran by just a few hundred yards in front of the car, cutting deep into the soil. They watched as the river carved a steep valley around them.

'The word today,' said Dad, 'is *highly informative and completely memorable geography lesson.*' He pressed harder on the Chronojuster, speeding time up just a little. Soft round hills rose up as though someone was inflating huge balloons beneath the soil.

Dad pulled the Chronojuster back and time slowed down. Meadows spread out around them.

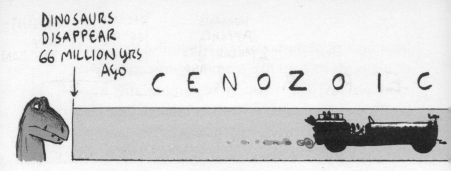

DINOSAURS
DISAPPEAR
66 MILLION yrs
AGO

C E N O Z O I C

A massive creature with a shaggy golden pelt shambled by without looking at them.

'Doggy! Doggy!' yelled Little Harry.

'In fact, it's megatherium,' said Lucy. 'We're in the age of the mammals, the Cenozoic. We're back in our own era.'

'Not far from home then,' said Dad.

'About another fifty million years,' said Lucy.

Time flies when you're enjoying yourself and the Tootings certainly enjoyed watching the river snuggle down among the new-made hills, and the thick deciduous forest gathering on their slopes. Herds of deer and buffalo thundered back and forth as the seasons flew by.

'I have to admit,' said Dad, 'I'm seeing a very different side to Basildon. Whoa! What was that?'

Somewhere above the forest he had glimpsed something amazing. He brought Chitty to a halt. Immediately everyone covered their ears. While

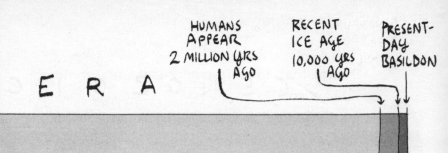

they had been travelling through time, everything was silent. Once they were still, they were bombarded with clattering, twittering birdsong.

'Look,' shouted Dad, 'I just spotted it out of the corner of my eye.'

A thin column of smoke was rising from a clearing somewhere down the valley.

'That's not a forest fire, that must be someone's bonfire. That's humans.'

'We can't be more than a couple of hundred thousand years from home,' said Lucy.

'We should go and say hello,' said Mum. 'It's only polite. After all, they are relatives.'

'No!' said Lucy. 'Think about it. What if we accidentally left a penknife or a box of matches behind? That could alter the course of human history. We might come home and find that the whole world had changed. Basildon might be full of people performing human sacrifice.'

'Or talking newts,' said Dad.

'What?'

'Newts that talk. It could happen. Anything could happen.'

Lucy's phone rang, playing an annnoyingly perky tune.

DWING ♫ DWING ♫ DIDDLE ᐳ BEEP! ᐸ FWAM FWAM

SNICK - SNICK - SNICK - SNICK

'How can the phone be ringing?' gasped Lucy. 'Phones won't be invented for tens of thousands of years. Electricity hasn't been invented yet. I'm not even sure that *talking*'s been invented.'

But the phone kept ringing. Louder and louder.

'Hello?' said Lucy.

'Helllllloooooooo,' purred a female voice. 'We seem to have missed you in traffic. But we don't want you to worry.'

Lucy froze. It was the voice of Nanny. The Nanny of notorious international supervillain Tiny Jack. The Nanny who just a few days ago had tried to steal Chitty and feed the children to her hungry piranhas.

'Nanny?' said Lucy, trying to be polite but almost choking in the process. 'How on earth—'

'These jelly phones – aren't they just marvellous?' cooed Nanny. 'You can call them wherever and whenever.'

'We're tens of thousands of years in the past,' said Lucy, amazed, putting her on speaker phone.

'Are you really? Well, don't worry. We can wait. We're quite comfortable where we are. Your front door very kindly put the kettle on the moment we opened it.' (Dad had done some DIY that caused the front door to greet guests and boil the kettle for tea.)

'Our front door?' hissed Mum. 'Where is she?'

'Thirteen Zborowski Terrace,' purred Nanny. 'It's soooo cosy. Jem, can you hear me? Tiny Jack is utterly delighted by your Scalextric. Oh, and Mr Tooting, I must say I'm very impressed by your collection of punctuality certificates . . .'

'My punctuality certificates were in my special box,' gasped Dad, 'under the bed.'

'That's right,' cooed Nanny. 'You're too modest. We're going to put them all on the wall for you, aren't we, Tiny Jack? We're going to decorate your room for you too, Lucy. It's so gloomy! We're going to brighten it up, aren't we, Tiny Jack?' She lowered her voice. 'The poor mite. He's so bored. I'm trying to keep him cheerful but what he really needs is someone to play with. Come home soon! We'll make sure the kettle is on!'

She hung up.

The Tootings looked at each other. The thought of Nanny and Tiny Jack poking around their house made them feel ill and angry and frightened all at the same time.

'The evil supervillain Tiny Jack!' exclaimed Mum. 'I was so busy escaping from stampeding dinosaurs I forgot all about the evil supervillain Tiny Jack!'

'And now he's got my punctuality certificates,' said Dad.

'My perfectly matt-very-black wallpaper,' sighed Lucy. 'Just when I'd got the room exactly how I like it.'

'Let's go straight home and throw them out,' said Mum.

'We can't just throw them out,' said Jem. 'They're evil supervillains. We're just an ordinary family from Basildon.'

'Ordinary family from Basildon!' snorted Mum. 'We just defeated a herd of ravening dinosaurs. We are the Mighty Tootings. And this is Chitty Chitty Bang Bang.'

'Exactly,' said Lucy. 'We've got Chitty Chitty

Bang Bang. Imagine what will happen if Tiny Jack gets her again, now that he knows she has a Chronojuster? If Tiny Jack had a time machine he could . . .'

'Steal all the gold in El Dorado,' said Mum.

'El Dorado is a myth,' said Lucy.

'The crown jewels, then,' said Jem, 'or the secret plans for the atomic bomb, or moon rockets, or fighter planes or . . . anything. If he gets Chitty he could travel back and forth through time doing anything he wants. Nobody would be safe. He could change the course of history. In the wrong hands Chitty Chitty Bang Bang is not just a fantastic car – she's a superweapon. Maybe we should stay here in the Stone Age.'

'We haven't packed for the Stone Age though,' said Dad. 'We've got no toothpaste. No soap. We'd probably need spears to catch our food . . .' He sighed. 'The word today is *it's all my fault*. If only I'd been content with the standard air-cooled flat-four 1.5-litre camper van. Why couldn't I have left Chitty's twenty-three-litre Maybach aero engine in the tree where I found it?'

'But then we wouldn't have had all this fun,' said Mum. 'Don't worry about it. Tiny Jack is just a little boy. All we have to do is go back to our time and I'll give him a good talking-to.'

'Will that really work?' asked Lucy. 'Last time we met he tried to feed us to piranhas.'

'Everyone has their off days,' said Mum.

'Maybe we could travel through time,' said Jem, 'and gather a band of heroes – Sherlock Holmes and Superman and maybe Sir Lancelot – and come back and defeat him.'

Lucy pointed out the one small problem with this plan. 'All of those people are fictional. Tiny Jack is real.'

'OK. What about Winston Churchill and Mahatma Gandhi?'

'Both so busy. Also they didn't really get on.'

'Plus the Chronojuster is quite sticky and hard to control. You might set out for 1945 and end up in 1845. Or we might set out to get Winston Churchill and end up with Hitler.'

'Surely you can fix that,' said Mum. 'You're so good at fixing things.'

'I don't know anything about how Chronojusters work. I'm not sure anyone does.'

'The Potts!' cried Jem. 'That's it. All we have to do is find the Potts.'

'What Potts?' said Mum.

'The Pott family. Commander Pott,' said Jem. 'Look, it's all here . . . in the logbook.'

The logbook of Chitty Chitty Bang Bang was

bound in soft, dark leather, inlaid with the Zborowski coat of arms (a dashing moustache sable on a field azur). Ever since Professor Tuk-Tuk gave it to him – thousands of

miles away and hundreds of years in the future – Jem had been carrying it around. He'd been so busy with dinosaur chases and the Ice Age that he hadn't really had time to share it with the others. Now he turned the pages carefully so the others could appreciate it. 'It's the whole story of Chitty Chitty Bang Bang's life. Look. Here are the races she won with Count Zborowski – the 1921 Lightning Short Handicap at Brooklands, the 1922 Lightning Short Handicap . . . then there's a burnt page. The book must have been in the car when she crashed. Then there's a gap. All these pages are damp and mouldy. That must be when she was left in the scrapyard. Then look. New people. The Pott family. The dad – Commander Pott of the Royal Navy. His wife, Mimsie. Their children, Jeremy and Jemima. And these pages are full of postcards and stamps from their travels – Calais, Egypt, South America, India. And look – in the back, all these drawings and diagrams. These are the plans for what they did to Chitty. Look, here's how the wings work. This one must be the time machine. This – "Monsieur Bon Bon's Secret Fooj Formula" – that must be to do with fuel. "Fooj" must be some kind of fuel.'

'Actually that's a recipe for fudge,' said Mum, reading over his shoulder. 'They just spelled it wrong.'

'The point is, it was the Potts who changed Chitty from a racing car into a submarine time machine that flies. They're geniuses. If anyone can help us defeat Tiny Jack, it's them.'

'This makes everything very simple,' said Lucy. 'Let's go.'

'Go where?' said Dad.

'Isn't it obvious?' said Lucy. 'We have to do three things. Number One: Find the Pott family. Jem, what was their last reported whereabouts?'

'1966.'

'1966,' mused Mum. 'The year that England won the football World Cup. Your dad would love to go there. Let's go.'

'Number Two: Explain to Mr Pott—'

'*Commander* Pott,' put in Jem. 'He was in the Navy.'

'We explain to Commander Pott that his great invention – Chitty Chitty Bang Bang – is in danger

32

of falling into the hands of an evil supervillain who could use it to destroy the whole world.'

'Oh, he'll be so annoyed about that.'

'Number Three: Ask him to give us one last ride in Chitty – back to our own time and our own house. And Number Four: Make him promise to go back to 1966 and uninvent Chitty.'

'*Uninvent Chitty?* You mean, let him take her away and never bring her back?' gasped Mum. 'But that means we can't have any more adventures! I was hoping to meet Marie Antoinette and the Queen of Sheba.'

'We should probably prioritize saving the world.'

'Wait a minute,' said Jem. 'If Commander Pott goes back to 1966 and uninvents Chitty, won't that mean Chitty never existed? And if she never existed, won't that mean that we don't just not have any more adventures, we won't have had the ones that we've had?'

'Say that again' said Dad.

'If we get back to our own time and he goes back to 1966 and uninvents Chitty, it will be impossible for us to have had our adventures, because we had them in Chitty and she will never have existed.'

'Interesting thought,' said Lucy.

'You're making my brain hurt,' said Dad.

'For instance, will Lucy still have film of the tyrannosaurs on her jelly phone?'

'Please stop,' said Dad.

'Are you saying we'll forget all about Chitty?' said Mum. 'Because I don't think I could stand that. With Chitty we're the Mighty Tootings but without her we're just some people from Basildon.'

'Some people from Basildon who saved the world,' said Dad. 'Ready, Tootings?'

'Ready, Dad,' said Lucy and Jem.

'I suppose,' shrugged Mum.

'Setting the course for 1966! Time for the Tootings to save the world.'

3

Dad slid the Chronojuster forward. The wind of time breeze whistled through the Tootings' bodies as they hurtled through history.

Dad's thought was: Will we have time to see the World Cup before we go off and save the world?

Mum's thought was: It'll be really interesting to see all those 1960s fashions – the short skirts, the long legs, the bright colours.

Lucy's thought was: It'll be really horrible looking at those 1960s fashions – the short skirts, the long legs, the bright colours.

Little Harry's thought was: Dinosaurs?

Jem's thought was: You can set a course for 1966, Dad, but in the end Chitty will take us wherever she wants to go. She's up to something and we need to know what.

All around them forests disappeared. Muddy tracks hardened into roads. Tall buildings rose up. The air filled with the sound of car horns and engines. Not the sweet, almost musical horns you find on modern cars but brash, deafening klaxons, like Chitty's. The engines were not quiet and efficient. They roared and growled in fury. Because Chitty had stalled in the middle of a road, snarling up the traffic. And what a road – a road that ran long and straight between buildings that were cliffs of glass and concrete. And what traffic – not boxy, tinny modern cars but great curving monsters gleaming with brass and steel and glossy leather. Cars with names like Packard, Pierce-Arrow and Cadillac. The drivers were not busy people with mobile phones and children, but men in fabulous suits with trilbies, women in cloche hats and fur coats, and chauffeurs in uniform.

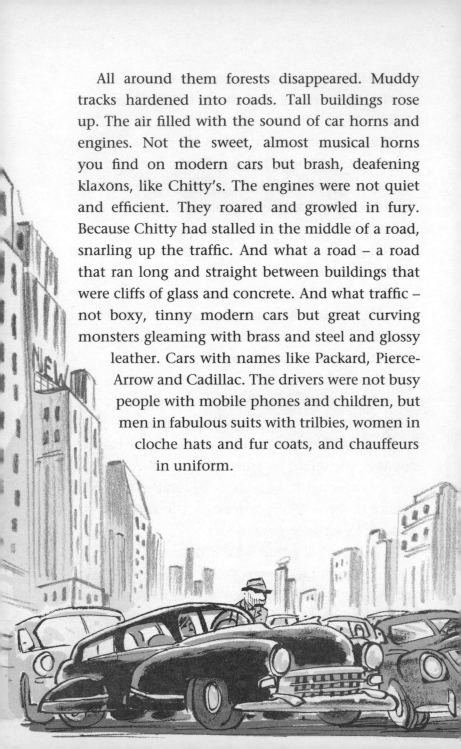

'Basildon has got so congested,' sighed Mum.

'I get the feeling that this is not Basildon,' said Jem.

'I get the feeling that this is not the twenty-first century,' said Lucy. 'Judging by the hats and cars, I'd say this was about 1926. Judging by the fact that that is clearly the Empire State Building I'd say we were in New York.'

'I'll get us out of here,' said Dad, jumping out and tugging at the crank handle.

'Why would you want to get out of New York in the 1920s?' said Mum, looking around in wonder at the shops, the coats, the architecture, the faces. 'Can't we stay a while?'

'I suppose going through the Ice Age has damaged the starter motor,' said Dad. 'And look at this . . . no wonder she won't start.' Great skeins of Cretaceous spider's web had got themselves wrapped around the crank shaft and now it wouldn't budge. Car horns honked louder. Drivers yelled more furiously. Dad got stressed.

'Don't get stressed,' said Mum.

Jem tried to help. He held the spanner, fetched the oil, apologized to the other drivers as he tried to unravel the prehistoric spider's web. It was surprisingly strong and sticky. It was just beginning to come lose when two immaculate leather shoes walked past him. A dashing young man with a curly moustache and a long silk scarf leaped gracefully on to Chitty's bonnet and put his hands in the air. 'Ladies and gentlemen of this New York,' he called in a rich, commanding English accent, 'do calm down. Yes, you are stuck in traffic. But is that such a terrible thing? You are at least stuck outside my house –' he waved his hand at a magnificent brick building, with a flight of steps rising up to the front door; in front of the door was a ridiculously tall butler in white tie and tails – 'which makes you my guests. Crackitt, crack it open!'

Crackitt must have been the name of the ridiculously tall butler. And what he cracked open was champagne. Gallons of it. From inside the magnificent house, a dozen or more neatly dressed young ladies came tap-dancing, all carrying bottles and glasses. In and out of the traffic they danced, pouring champagne for the motorists and passengers. But it wasn't the dancers or the champagne that interested Jem. It was the young man in the scarf. He had seen him before somewhere, or at least a picture of him. 'Don't look on this as a traffic jam!' he was crying. 'Think of it as an unexpected party.' Then he looked down at Jem and at the hank of sticky white stuff he was holding. 'I say,' he said. 'What on earth is that?'

'It's prehistoric spider's web,' explained Jem. 'Amazingly strong and quite sticky. Chitty got caught up in one this morning – or sixty-six million years ago, depending on how you look at it. Our car can travel back in time.'

'Can she really? Extraordinary. No use to me, of course. I'm more interested in going forward in time – towards the finishing line.'

Suddenly Jem knew where he had seen the man. 'Are you,' he asked, 'by any chance are you . . . Count Zborowski?'

'The very same,' smiled the Count, bowing his head. 'My compliments on your rather magnificent car. A Paragon Panther if I'm not mistaken.'

'That's right,' said Jem. He patted Chitty's gleaming wheel arch and thought, I don't know why you brought us here, Chitty, but I do know it's not a coincidence that you stalled outside the house of your first owner.

'I had a Panther myself,' said the Count. 'I was reliably informed she was the only one of her kind. But perhaps my informer was not as reliable as I thought.'

'No, no,' said Jem. 'This is her. This is your car. This is Chitty Chitty Bang Bang.'

'That can't be quite right, you know,' said the Count. 'I was racing my Chitty at Brooklands – Lightning Short Handicap, 1922 – and I'm afraid the dear old thing went stark staring bonkers, drove straight through the timing hut, dashed near killed me. Completely wrecked herself.'

'That's her,' said Mum. 'The very same Chitty Chitty Bang Bang.'

'Dad restored her to her former beauty,' said Jem proudly.

'Even though I'm talking,' said the Count, 'I'm speechless. Really. I have no idea what to say. She looks even more beautiful now than she did when she was new. Sir, you must surely be the finest mechanic in the world.'

'Well,' said Dad, 'if I were really that good, we wouldn't be having all this trouble getting her started.'

'Step aside,' said the Count. 'I have a wrinkle for Chitty's engine that works on even the coldest morning. Crackitt!'

Crackitt passed the Count a short sword and a bottle of champagne. The Count took the bottle in one hand and the sword in the other and with a single, sweeping gesture he sliced through the neck of the bottle, as easily as if it had been made of butter. Champagne gurgled out, bubbling over Chitty's bonnet.

'Oh!' gasped Mum, impressed. Lucy and Jem applauded but, more importantly, Chitty's engine spluttered. 'Give the starter a shove, Jem.'

Jem jumped into the driver's seat and tried Chitty's starter motor. Her splutter turned into a roar. The Count placed his hand on the bonnet. The roar turned to a purr, as if Chitty recognized the touch of her favourite hand in all the world.

'Hear that?' yelled Dad. 'The word today is

we are back on the road again.'

'Champagne,' said the Count. 'An infallible cure for engine trouble. Has to be a good year, of course. This is the '98. Chitty was always very particular about her champagne. Chin-chin, by the way . . .' He took a gulp of the champagne and then offered the bottle first to Mum and then to Lucy.

A strange sound like a mouse being strangled came from somewhere inside Lucy. Jem, Mum and even Little Harry stared at her. She'd never made a sound like this before.

'Lucy,' said Mum, 'I know this sounds unlikely . . . Did you just giggle?'

'I have never giggled in my life,' said Lucy, narrowing her eyes, 'and you know that.'

'Oh, but what a shame! You do it so dashed nicely,' smiled the Count, taking another gulp of champagne.

The strangled-mouse sound came from inside Lucy once more.

'You just did it again!' said Mum. 'You are definitely giggling.'

'I'm not giggling,' growled Lucy, 'I'm thinking. For instance, I'm thinking . . . If this is New York in 1926, then alcohol is illegal.'

'Oh,' said the Count, 'dash it. I always forget champagne is alcohol.'

A little way further up Broadway, the yowl of sirens split the air. It was the sound of the New York City Police Department coming to arrest someone for distributing gallons of hooch. Up and down Broadway, the other motorists threw away their glasses, leaped into their cars, chewed mints, and tried to act like they'd never touched a drop.

'What a dashed nuisance,' said the Count. 'I'm going to be carted off to jail for the rest of my natural, just as I was going to drive the most important race of my life.'

Then, 'Chitty, Chitty,' said Chitty's engine.

And, 'Bang, Bang,' said her exhaust.

Chitty Chitty Bang Bang was ready to go.

The Count leaped in next to Jem. 'How are you at getaway driving?' he said.

The sirens were louder now, but they were almost drowned out by the revving of the other cars' engines, the sounding of their horns, the yelling of their drivers, all desperate for Chitty to move so that they could get away from the police.

Before Jem could explain that Dad was the driver and that he was only in the driving seat in order to press the starter button, Chitty barged away from the kerb and roared off down Broadway.

'Wait!' called Dad, who was still on the pavement. Chitty, of course, did not wait but she *did* swerve to miss a fire hydrant, giving Dad just enough time to jump aboard as she swung around the corner into West 31st Street.

'Smooth work,' smiled the Count, ruffling Jem's hair.

'It's not me, it's the car,' said Jem, clinging on to Chitty's steering wheel, hypnotized with fear as pedestrians and red lights whizzed past. But Chitty's engine drowned out everything he said.

'Bang! Bang!' yelled Little Harry.

'Yes,' cooed Mum. 'Chitty Chitty Bang Bang.'

'Bang! Bang! Bang!' insisted Little Harry.

He's not talking about the car, thought Jem. I wonder, what is he talking about?

'Bang! Bang! Bang! Bang!' yelled Little Harry and just then a swarm of bullets buzzed past Jem's head like furious wasps.

'Trouble ahead!' called the Count. Two police cars were powering towards them, lights flashing. 'By the way, they seem to be shooting at us.'

Jem tried to keep hold of the wheel but it spun out of his hands as the car swung left and then right.

'What a nuisance,' sighed the Count. He poked his head up and shouted at the police, 'I say! Be careful, can't you! You've burst our front tyre!' Then he turned to Jem and said, 'Would you mind driving her on two wheels? You know, sort of tip her on the side and keep her steady as she goes?'

Before Jem could speak, Chitty lurched over to one side, brakes screaming for mercy as she shimmied on to Fifth Avenue, on her two left wheels, her two right wheels up in the air.

'Perfect,' smiled the Count, clambering out on to the side of the car, crawling along her bodywork towards the rear wheel.

'What are you doing?' yelled Mum.

The Count balanced on the running-board, bullets whistling round his head. 'It's not too sticky once you get the hang of it,' he yelled back. 'Just like surfing. Except for the bullets, of course. Keep her up on two wheels, old chap, while I change the tyre.'

The Tooting family watched in awe as the Count removed Chitty's back tyre while hurtling along Fifth Avenue at full speed. 'Did it all the time at Brooklands,' he said. 'Can't afford to stop to change tyres when you're in a race, you know. Have to do it while you're on the move. There she goes.' He pulled the flat tyre off and hurled it from the back of Chitty, towards the police cars. Swerving to miss it, the police cars rammed into each other. 'That'll teach them to shoot at a chap while he's doing his car maintenance. Now, where's the spare?' Within a few seconds, the Count had the new tyre fitted and was back on the passenger seat next to Jem. 'Drive on all fours wheels now,' he said. 'Faster that way.'

Just as he said this a pair of police motorcycles flew out of the side streets, sirens blasting. They raced along, one each side of Chitty.

'Couldn't we just stop and explain?' said Mum.

'Explain what?' said Dad.

'That we didn't know about their alcohol laws because we have come from the future via the late Cretaceous period.'

The riders crouched over their engines, gripping their handlebars with massive leather gauntlets, staring into Chitty with their goggled eyes. They didn't look like they were interested in explanations.

'Trouble is,' said the Count, 'this is not the first time I've forgotten about the No Champagne law. Last time, I believe the electric chair was mentioned as a distinct possibility. Best head for the river.'

'Why?' said Dad.

'The river is absolutely the only place to go when you're in lumber with the law,' said the Count. 'Head for the river, I always say. Not sure why, but it has a ring to it, don't you think?'

'What river?' said Jem.

'Not sure what they call it,' said the Count. 'But

it's a jolly fine river. Just at the bottom of East 79th.'

'That's the Hudson River,' said Lucy. 'The official border between New York City and New Jersey.'

Chitty was already spinning on her back wheels, skidding into East 79th, rushing towards the Hudson River. Jem could see the funnel of a ferry boat and the dazzle of wide, cold water.

'You might want to brake now,' said the Count. 'River's coming towards us a little bit quickly . . .'

Jem could see an esplanade. An old man was feeding the seagulls. A family was looking over the metal railing, waving at passing boats. He tried to press the brake but the brake seemed to press back.

'I honestly would brake now,' said the Count, leaning back in his seat. 'If you drive into fences too quickly, they break. I know because I've done it.'

'Jem! Brake!' yelled Dad.

'Fasten your seat belts!' yelled Jem. No matter what Jem did, he couldn't make Chitty turn left or right. She was heading straight for the railings. 'We're just going to have to trust Chitty.'

'Bang!' banged Chitty as one of the police motorcycles tore ahead and dodged in front of her, trying to force her to slow down.

'Bang!' banged Chitty as she stopped as suddenly as if she had hit a brick wall. The police motorcycle in front tore into the distance without noticing that Chitty wasn't following. The police motorcycle behind tried to swerve but too late, and hit Chitty's huge chrome bumper side on. It spun round and round on its back wheel, blue smoke billowing from its tyres. Finally it toppled gently on to its side. The rider tried to stand up but all that spinning had made him too dizzy.

The Count turned to Lucy. 'What ho,' he said.

'What ho,' said Lucy, who wasn't sure what the polite response to 'What ho' was.

'What ho, ho,' said the Count.

'What?' said Lucy.

'Conversation not my strong point, I'm afraid,' said the Count. 'Especially with ladies of the opposite sex. I'm all right as far as "What ho" and then I tend to get stuck.'

'Very nice to meet you,' said Lucy.

'Corking great coincidence strolling into you on Broadway like that.'

A coincidence, thought Jem, is exactly what this is not. Chitty wants to be here for some reason.

Before he had time to think about that reason, a storm of blue light flickered across the esplanade. Police cars. A fleet of them. Lined up across the bottom of the street, like a troop of cavalry, ready to charge.

'Well, toodle-oo,' said the Count. 'Perhaps I'll run.' He tried to undo his seat belt but it seemed to be stuck and when he tried to slide out from under it, he seemed only to get more stuck.

Without even noticing himself doing it, Jem found that he had placed his foot on the accelerator. Such a nice, comfortable accelerator, so perfectly designed to fit your foot. You just had to press it. The handbrake, too, the way its ebony handle fitted so snugly and warmly into your hand, you just wanted to lift it up and let it . . . It was as though Chitty was whispering to him, persuading him to let her go. She was so difficult to say no to. Jem let slip the handbrake. Jem pressed the accelerator. Chitty rushed towards the blockade of police cars.

'Brake!' yelled the Count.

Chitty barged the police cars aside and tore across the esplanade.

'Brake! Brake!' yelled Dad.

The Count covered his eyes as the metal barrier splintered all around them.

'Actually . . .' said Lucy as the car tumbled off the quay.

'In fact . . .' she said as the freezing water rushed up to meet them.

'I think . . .' she went on as Chitty rushed through the cold air. 'I think you're going to like this.'

4

Detective Finbar O'Shaunessy had joined the New York City Police Department in 1901 when he was sixteen years old. For twenty-five years he had walked the streets of Manhattan, upholding the law. He'd dealt with robbers and riots, gangsters and gangs. He'd arrested a man who claimed he could saw the island of Manhattan in half. He'd seen Houdini escape from a straitjacket while dangling from a crane high above the river. He'd seen a man jump off the Brooklyn Bridge and survive. He'd met Charlie Chaplin and Babe Ruth. But in all that time he'd never seen anything as surprising as what he saw on the esplanade that afternoon. A big jalopy of a racing car with a little kid at the wheel had smashed through the barrier and bellyflopped into the cold, black waters of the Hudson. Detective

O'Shaunessy had taken off his hat. He believed it was important to show respect when people died – even if they were bootleggers and joyriders. But the car didn't sink! It rocked unsteadily for a moment on the waves, then swung its bonnet round in the direction of Liberty Island and began to chug across the river and out of his jurisdiction.

'What in the name of Liberty . . . ?' said Detective O'Shaunessy, who did not know that under the waves, the wheels of Chitty Chitty Bang Bang were realigning themselves until they were all pointing backwards. They turned, churning the water like propellers. Too confused to think, the detective waved his hat at them.

'What an absolute corker of a car!' said the Count. 'I must say I had no idea she could float.'

As if she had heard him, Chitty's engine went from churning to spinning as quick as a heart can leap, and the car sped through the water, shooting spray from her prow. The Tootings waved merrily from the back seat as she carved a great bow wave through the bay.

'I say,' said the Count. 'You really have done a marvellous job on her, Mr Tooting.'

'I don't know about that,' said Dad modestly. 'The fact is we've been having a bit of trouble with the Chronojuster. It seems to be stuck. You don't have any handy hints about that, do you? Would champagne work maybe?'

'What's a Chronojuster?'

'The Chronojuster is the thing that makes her travel through time.'

'Never heard of it. She didn't travel through time in my day. You couldn't sail her either. All I knew was that she went really fast. I seem to have underestimated the dear old girl. I couldn't take a turn behind the wheel, I don't suppose? For old times' sake?'

The sound of Chitty's engine deepened from chugging to purring. Instead of bouncing over the waves, she cut smoothly through them, as though inviting the Count into the driving seat. Jem shuffled out from behind the wheel. The Count stood up.

'Do you have a new car now?' asked Lucy. 'A safer one?'

'I don't know about safer. She's certainly faster,' said the Count, as he clambered over Jem. 'Guess what I named her? Pretty clever actually. I called her Chitty Chitty Bang Bang . . . the Second. There. What d'you think? Got a bit of a ring to it, wouldn't you say?'

The moment he said this, Chitty's engine stopped purring and started roaring, and Chitty went from gliding back to bouncing through the waves. Lucy grabbed the Count's hand as he struggled to keep his balance. Dad tried to reach the brakes but it was no good. With a terrible splash the Count tumbled into the dark, freezing water.

'Quick! A rope!' called Lucy, afraid that the Count might be left to drown as the car sped away. But as soon as the Count hit the water, Chitty's engine cut out. She rocked idly on the waves, making a low, watery, stuttering noise that sounded for all the world like a chuckle.

'See?' said the Count as, shivering and dripping, he struggled back on board. 'She does have a temper.'

They wrapped the Count in towels and blankets and used the heat from the pistons to brew him a mug of hot chocolate, while Chitty sailed upriver.

'Ice cream! Ice cream!' yelled Little Harry, pointing ahead.

'Too cold for ice cream, darling,' said Mum.

'Ice cream! Ice cream!' insisted Little Harry.

'Too cold,' said Mum, but Jem thought, Little Harry is always right. He looked where his brother was pointing – and there, pale and cloudy against the sunset, rising up from the waters, was the colossal figure of a woman; on her head was a

crown and in her hand – raised above her head –
was what seemed to be a gigantic ice-cream cone.

'That's actually the Torch of Freedom,' explained
Lucy, 'not an ice cream. We are looking at the
Statue of Liberty.'

As they watched, a fat full moon ballooned
up behind the statue's head, like a silver speech
bubble, flushing the giant face with moonlight.
Music drifted towards them over the water, as
though Liberty herself were singing. Someone was
having a party at the base of the statue. Chitty
puttered up to the Liberty Island landing stage and
the Count led them all ashore, saying, 'Say what
you like about Chitty, she could always sniff out a
good party!'

At the base of the Statue of Liberty is a kind of
fort. That night it was covered in fairy lights and
pulsing with piano music. The shadows of dancers
flickered across every window. A couple of elegant
young men in beautiful suits were chatting in the
doorway. They seemed delighted to see the Count.

'Count Zborowski!'

'Count Basie!' said the Count. 'Tootings, this
gentleman is the finest piano player in New York.'

'In fact I'm not even the finest piano player in
this doorway,' smiled Count Basie. 'Allow me to
introduce Duke Ellington.'

'Count Zborowski,' said the Duke.

'Duke,' said the Count.

'I hope you are in good shape for the big race tomorrow,' said the Duke, 'as I have a large bundle of dough riding on your victory.'

'Duke,' said Count Basie, 'have you not heard? This very afternoon the Count drove with such skill that he left the entire New York City Police Department for dust and escaped across the river.'

'With a driver of such skill, my money is safe,' said the Duke.

'As a matter of fact,' said the Count, 'I wasn't driving. It was my young friend Jem Tooting here. Finest getaway driver in the business.'

'Well, friends, here we have an excellent reason to celebrate,' said Count Basie. 'Let us step inside and dance.'

'Oh! Yes!' said Lucy. All the other Tootings stared at her.

'But you hate dancing,' said Dad.

'And it's been an unusually long day,' said Mum.

'Sixty-six million years long, to be precise,' said Dad. 'I think we're too tired for music.'

'You know,' said the Duke, 'everything is music. Out here in the cold we have the music of the waves, the music of the gulls, the music of the sea breezes and, if you listen close, the music of the spheres. Indoors we have the music of Duke Ellington. Just another music. Only my music is indoors and warm, and accompanied by fine food.'

'We *are* hungry,' said Mum.

'Just for five minutes then,' said Dad.

As they walked through the doors, a lady with hair like candyfloss and lips the colour of raspberry sauce came at them with a silver tray. 'Ice cream, anyone?' she said.

Little Harry really is always right, thought Jem.

Ripples of melody and thrills of rhythm filled the air. Champagne corks popped. Girls giggled. Cigarette smoked drifted and candlelight blushed. There were men in loud check jackets with scars on their faces. Girls in dresses covered in beads and feathers, with bobbed hair and sparkly shoes. And the strangest thing to Jem and Lucy was that everyone knew how to dance. There was no embarrassing shuffling or stomping. People turned and spun and clapped in time to the music and in perfect tune with each other. This was the first time Lucy had ever been to a party that didn't involve pass-the-parcel and cake. It was the most fabulously beautiful event she'd ever seen. Up on the stage, Count Zborowski was speaking into a microphone.

'Ladies, gentlemen and especially Tootings,' he said. 'Tomorrow I shall be racing in the greatest motor race in the world – the Prix d'Esmerelda's Birthday Cake. I had a new car built specially for the race and a jolly fine car she is too, with a jolly fine name for her – Chitty Chitty Bang Bang the Second. Until now, I have not had a mechanic. Tonight that has changed. Tonight I have found the greatest motor mechanic in the history of the world . . . not just a great mechanic, but a great inventor . . . Mr Tooting.'

All the lights went out apart from one big spotlight which was trained on Dad. The crowd cheered. Applauded. Slapped him on the back. Dad looked uncomfortable.

'Speech!' cried everyone.

'The word today,' mumbled Dad, 'is *I can't think of a word to say.*'

'I'll pay you heaps of money,' promised the Count. 'And there'll be heaps of food.'

'Thing is,' said Dad, thinking sadly of the day he lost his job at Very Small Parts For Very Big Machines, 'I've got these fat fingers . . .'

But no one heard him over the cheers and applause.

'You'll be marvellous,' said Mum, pinching Dad's cheek. 'I've always thought Grand Prix racing would suit you. Let's dance.'

Jem and Lucy watched in horror as their parents moved towards the dance floor. Surely they weren't going to dance?

'What are we doing here?' groaned Lucy.

'I was just wondering that myself,' said Jem. 'Think about it. All the time we thought we were driving Chitty it turned out she was driving us.

Taking us all over the world to collect her old spare parts. She took us to the Cretaceous period to escape from Tiny Jack. Now she's brought us here. There must be a reason.'

'The reason,' said Lucy, 'is obvious.' She was watching the dancers closely, wondering if she could learn the steps. 'Or it will be when you're older.'

'Lucy, what are you talking about?'

'Chitty is in love with the Count.'

'What? Why would she be in love with the Count?'

'Because he's handsome and dashing. He hands out champagne to strangers and he knows all these other counts and dukes and he takes us to parties.'

'She's a car. Why would a car be in love with a man? Why would a car want to go to parties? Wouldn't a car be in love with another car?'

'Cars don't fall in love with cars. They fall in love with drivers. The Count drove Chitty to all her greatest triumphs. They won cups and prizes together. People poured champagne on her bonnet. She misses him. She loves him. She wants him back. It's not easy to find a man as brave and stylish as the Count . . .'

'Hem, hem,' said Jem, nodding his head meaningfully at Lucy. She looked behind her and there was the Count, standing right at her shoulder. Had he heard all the things she'd said about him being handsome and dashing and brave? Lucy felt hot and embarrassed.

'What ho,' said the Count, glancing at the dance floor and taking a deep breath. Oh no, thought Lucy, he's going to ask me to dance and I don't know how to dance but I really would like to dance. 'What . . .' said Lucy, 'oh . . .'

The 'ho' came out as an 'oh' because she had just seen the Worst Thing She Had Seen All Day. Worse than rampaging dinosaurs threatening her baby brother, worse than the New York City Police Department shooting at her, worse than plunging into the Hudson River – she saw . . . her parents dancing.

Why? Why? *Why?* Why were they dancing? They didn't have a clue! They tried to copy the other dancers but they kept bumping heads and stepping on each other's toes. Somehow, instead of this making them want to die of embarrassment, it was making them laugh and . . . Oh no. They had their arms around each other. They were going to smooch.

'I wonder,' said the Count, 'if I could interest you in a little . . .'

'Sorry,' said Lucy. 'Got to put Little Harry to bed.'

She grabbed Little Harry and headed for the exit.

'Me too,' said Jem.

'What,' said the Count, as they vanished into the crowd, 'ho.'

Jem and Lucy didn't like Mum and Dad's dancing but all the other guests were crazy about it. In New York in 1926 no one had seen anyone twist and shake like Dad before. Everyone wanted to copy it. An amazingly beautiful woman called Josephine Baker was the first to learn. She called the dance 'The Toot' in honour of the Tootings. Seven minutes later everyone on Liberty Island was doing the Toot. Seven days later everyone in Manhattan was doing it. Seven weeks later everyone in America was tooting. And seven months later, they were tooting in Brisbane and Belfast and Bali.

On the dance floor, Mum and Dad were surrounded by young people asking them to show them the steps.

'No, no,' said Mum. 'He has to go and lie down.

After all, he's in the big race tomorrow.'

'But I'm having such a good time,' said Dad.

'Me too,' smiled Mum.

Jem was just about to step outside when a hairy hand with manicured nails and a big diamond ring grabbed him. At the end of the hand was a muscular arm. At the end of the arm was a broad, solid shoulder and on top of the shoulder was a head with carefully brushed hair and a smile wide enough to hang washing from. The smile was unusually twinkly . . . How could any smile be that twinkly? thought Jem.

'If it is no bother,' said the owner of the smile, 'I would like you to make my acquaintance. I am known hereabouts as Mr Lenny Manmountain.'

'Diamonds!' said Jem, who had finally worked out what made the smile so twinkly: every one of Lenny Manmountain's teeth had a diamond in the middle.

'Well, Mr Diamonds, I hear about how you leave

the New York City Police Department for dust today in your amphibious automobile, and I admit, I am most impressed.'

'Thanks,' said Jem. He was about to explain that his name was not Diamonds but Tooting, when Mr Manmountain turned to the beautiful young woman with the candyfloss hair and the tangfastic lips.

'This,' he said, pointing to Jem, 'is Mr Diamonds, the celebrated getaway driver.'

'Oh,' squealed the beautiful woman, 'let me give him a big lipsticky kiss!' As she peeled her lipsticky lips from his cheek, Jem found he suddenly no longer felt the need to say his name wasn't Diamonds, or that he was just a little boy from Basildon and not a New York getaway driver.

'I am most surprised by the youngness of his age,' said the beautiful young woman. 'It is impressive that he achieves so much in such a short life.'

'This is true,' said Mr Manmountain. 'Mr Diamonds, if ever you wish to make a large amount of money by using your getaway driving skills to help me avoid the unwelcome attentions of the police, I will most certainly hire you.'

'Sure,' muttered Jem in a voice that he thought suggested that he was getting offers like this all the time. 'Why not?'

*

Down at the jetty Lucy was putting Little Harry to bed on Chitty's back seat. She wrapped him in a thick fleecy tartan rug and made a pillow of his little red backpack. It felt heavier than usual and so full it wouldn't zip up properly.

'What have you got in there?' said Lucy.

'Dinosaur,' said Little Harry, stuffing it under the blanket.

'So that's where you're keeping your remote-control dinosaur? OK. You keep it nice and warm under there. And you can use my coat for a pillow.'

Just as Little Harry was nodding off to sleep, a voice said, 'What ho!' The Count leaned over the running-board, and smiled at Lucy.

'Oh. Don't you like the party?'

'It's an absolute corker of a party. I just thought I'd volunteer to do a spot of lookout duty.'

'Lookout duty?'

'The party is stuffed to the rafters with criminal types and illegal hooch. Someone has to look out for the police. I tend to do that because everyone else likes to talk. I like to talk too, of course, but I tend to get a bit stuck once I've said, "What ho!"'

'I see.'

'What ho, by the way.'

'What ho to you too. Are Mum and Dad coming out soon?'

'Gracious, no,' said the Count. 'They're the toast of New York. They seem to have invented this new dance. Would you like me to teach it to you?'

'Not now,' said Lucy. 'Or ever.'

'Just looking out, then,' said the Count. 'Perhaps you'd like to look out too?'

Lucy and the Count sat in comfortable silence on Chitty's long, warm bonnet. A faraway ferry sounded its hooter. The great cliff of the Statue of Liberty towered above them. Cascades of moonlight flowed down the folds of her skirts.

'Makes you wonder,' said the Count.

'Wonder what?'

'Who she is. How she got there. Who built her.'

'Who built who?'

'The Statue of Liberty. Look at her. She's dashed enigmatic, isn't she? Keeping the jolly old secrets of her origin and her significance to herself. She is a mystery mankind will never really solve.'

'The Statue of Liberty,' said Lucy, 'was designed by the sculptor Frédéric Bartholdi. It was a gift from the people of France to the people of America on the occasion of the centenary of American Independence. Made in France, it was shipped in pieces and assembled here on Liberty Island. When the pieces arrived they were driven through New York and given a ticker-tape parade. Bartholdi originally

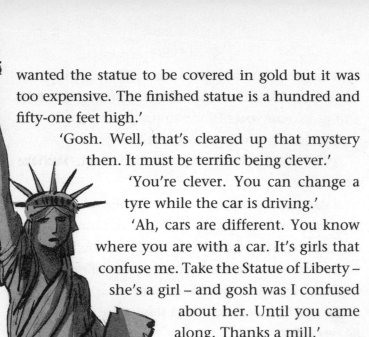

wanted the statue to be covered in gold but it was too expensive. The finished statue is a hundred and fifty-one feet high.'

'Gosh. Well, that's cleared up that mystery then. It must be terrific being clever.'

'You're clever. You can change a tyre while the car is driving.'

'Ah, cars are different. You know where you are with a car. It's girls that confuse me. Take the Statue of Liberty – she's a girl – and gosh was I confused about her. Until you came along. Thanks a mill.'

'Anything else I can help you with?'

'Do you happen to know anything about girls that aren't a hundred and fifty-one feet high and made of copper?'

'I am a girl.'

'So you are. Now if you were a different girl – for instance, the one with the red lips and the candyfloss hair – speaking as a girl, what would you say to her if you were a chap?'

LUCY
&
COUNT Z
↓

'I might say, "Nice to meet you", but I prefer someone dark and intelligent and a little mysterious and not so obvious.'

'Really? And you think she'll like that?'

'Why don't you just say, "Hello, would you like to dance?"'

'I can't really dance.'

'Then just say, "Hello."'

'What if she laughs in my face?'

'Why would she do that? You know, she might be in there right now thinking, *That Count Zborowski, he's so dashing and brave and handsome, why doesn't he ever talk to me?*'

'Do girls have thoughts like that?'

'Of course they do.'

'Extraordinary. That's exactly the type of thoughts that chaps have.'

'Girls or boys – everyone is just people.'

'You know, I think I'll jolly well give it a shot.'

The Count went back to the party. Thirty seconds later, he left the party with the girl with the candyfloss hair holding on to his arm. 'Jolly excellent advice, Lucy,' he called. 'You'll never guess what . . .'

But the girl with the candyfloss hair didn't give her time to guess. She just blurted it out, 'Count Louis and me are gonna be married!'

'*Married?*'

'I'm so excited. I am never married before in all my long life. Except that one time. But that was in Arkansas. Also that was months ago. And who remembers that far back?'

'Not me, certainly,' said the Count.

'OK.' said the bride-to-be. 'Let's go to church!'

'You're going now?' gasped Lucy. 'But I thought you were about to drive in the Greatest Motor Race in the World.'

'Crikey, the Prix d'Esmerelda's Birthday Cake! I completely forgot,' gasped the Count. 'I say, you wouldn't care to get married after the race, I don't suppose?'

'But, Louis! We've already told all these people . . .' People were pouring out of the party: Duke Ellington, Count Basie, Josephine Baker, Mum, Dad, Mr Manmountain. They were all standing on the jetty, waiting to wave off the happy couple. 'I want to go now. I'm going crazy waiting here,' said the bride-to-be.

'There's no ferry until morning,' said Lucy.

'That's exactly why it's so fortunate that your car is amphibious. Where's Diamonds? Diamonds is going to drive us.'

'Who is Diamonds?' asked Dad, surprised to hear that someone else was going to drive his car.

'That would be me,' muttered Jem, blushing as he stepped out from behind Dad.

'Oh no,' said Dad. 'You're too young to drive. This is a big city.'

'But Diamonds is the finest getaway driver in New York!' wailed the bride-to-be. 'Please say yes. This is my happy day.'

'Why would anyone need a getaway driver for a wedding?' asked Lucy.

'So we can "get away" on our honeymoon, of course.'

'But you can't just get married,' said Mum. 'What about all the nice things – wedding dresses, confetti, bridesmaids . . .'

'My mother told me, "Always be ready for anything, especially anything romantic,"' said the bride-to-be, producing from her huge handbag a gorgeous silk damask wedding dress. 'If you'll all just look away for a moment, I'll wriggle into this. Especially you, Louis. It's bad luck to see the bride before the wedding.'

Within seconds she was transformed into the perfect bride, complete with cloud-coloured dress, ivory veil and a bouquet of snowdrops. 'And look what I found!' she gasped, brandishing a fistful of very, very pink cloth at Lucy. 'The perfect bridesmaid dress for the little lady.'

'Oh no,' said Lucy. 'Oh no, no, no, no, no, no. No!'

'Oh but Lucy,' pleaded Mum, 'it's lovely.'

'Mum, I've seen the back end of a pterodactyl and the front end of a megatherium. But I have never seen anything half as horrible as that dress.'

The bride-to-be began to cry big, mascara-smudging tears. 'Ever since I am a little girl in Little Rock, all I want is pretty bridesmaids on my wedding day. That is all I ask.'

The Count began to panic. 'Lucy,' he said, 'help. You know all about girls. This one is crying. I don't know what to do. Can you make it stop?'

'I'll wear the dress,' groaned Lucy.

'Really?' cooed the bride-to-be. 'I do believe my mother will be so proud when she sees how prepared I am. Why, here I even have ribbons to decorate the car. And . . . all sorts of other things that may be useful.'

As she said this last sentence, Jem saw her wink at Manmountain.

Dad would only agree to let Jem drive if he could sit in the front passenger seat alongside him. They set off into the bay, with Chitty's ribbons flying and Lucy's ribbons stuck firmly in her mouth as she sucked them angrily while Mum tied her hair into tight, tiny braids, each one fastened with a little gemstone butterfly.

'What do you think?' asked Mum, showing her herself in a mirror.

'You made my hair look like spaghetti infested with insects.'

Out in the bay, the wind and seagulls were louder. Jem whispered to his Dad, 'There's something very strange here.'

'Yes, what is it? It's very sticky,' said Dad, who had put his foot on the roll of prehistoric spider's web.

'I'm not talking about that,' hissed Jem. 'That's prehistoric spider's web. I'm talking about this so-called wedding.'

Dad bundled up the spider's web and tossed it on to the back seat.

'Sticky!' yelled Little Harry, patting it enthusiastically.

'Oh, Little Harry! Now I'll have to untangle you,' sighed Dad.

'Dad, listen. Why would they get married if they've only just met?'

'Haven't you heard of love at first sight?'

'Why is Manmountain carrying a violin case?'

'Because he plays the violin?' said Dad.

'How can he play the violin? He's got big fat fingers.'

'Are you saying,' growled Dad, 'that there is something wrong with fat fingers?'

'No, no,' said Jem quickly. 'I'm saying there's something strange going on here.'

By now they had crossed the bay and trundled on to the jetty and into the streets of Little Italy. It was early morning. Street sweepers were cleaning the pavements and traders were piling their stalls with fresh fruit and vegetables. Seeing a beautiful car with a bride in the back, the sweepers waved their brushes in the air. Whenever Jem had to stop at a traffic light or a road junction, the stallholders came with bags of sugared almonds for the bride and the children. One of them even sang to her.

'*Che bella sposa,*' he sang.

'How romantic,' sighed the bride-to-be, singing along.

Determined to find out exactly what was going on, Jem looked at her in the rear-view mirror and said, 'I was just wondering . . . What's your name?'

'That's exactly what I was wondering!' gasped the Count. 'Darling, what's your name?'

The bride-to-be's eyes narrowed.

Lenny Manmountain growled, 'What? You didn't hear what the stallholder guy said? Her name is Bella Sposa.'

Lucy pointed out that 'Bella Sposa' was just Italian for 'Beautiful Bride-to-Be'.

'Well, quelle coincidence,' smiled Bella Sposa.

'Bella Sposa is what I am called and Bella Sposa is exactly what I am.'

'How charmingly uncomplicated,' smiled the Count.

'Thank you,' said Bella. 'I think you're uncomplicated too.'

The Count looked happier than ever when she said this. Even Mum said, 'Aaaah!' and Bella Sposa kept singing that song. 'After all,' she said, 'not everyone has a song named after them.' Jem, though, was more supicious than ever.

'Mr Manmountain,' he said, as they drove into Brooklyn, 'I bet Bella would love it if you accompanied her on the violin.'

'Bet?' said Manmountain. 'How big a bet? I don't bet on anything under two gees.'

'I didn't mean actual money. I was just using a figure of speech.'

'When it comes to figures, cash is better than speech,' said Manmountain. 'Every time.'

The Brooklyn streets were full of schoolchildren. They ran after Chitty, daring each other to jump up on her running-board.

'Look at the beautiful car!' they cried.

'Ga gooo ga!' answered Chitty.

'Look at the beautiful bride!'

Bella Sposa waved at them all.

A boy with very bright red hair jumped up on Chitty's running-board, right beside the Count. 'Hey, mister! New York's finest shoeshine for your big day – ten cents?'

'Oh, my!' gasped Bella. 'Look at his hair. It goes so well with the bridesmaid's dress. What's your name, kid?'

'Red,' said the kid. 'Like my hair.'

'Such decorative hair. Climb in and you can be my pageboy.'

'OK, lady. It'll cost you a dollar, though.'

'Wait,' said Mum. 'Hasn't your mother told you never to get into a car with strangers?'

'Sure, but my grandma told me there was no such thing as strangers, only friends we haven't met yet. Dollar, lady?'

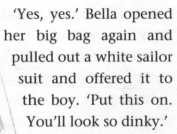

'Yes, yes.' Bella opened her big bag again and pulled out a white sailor suit and offered it to the boy. 'Put this on. You'll look so dinky.'

'You never mentioned no sailor suit before, lady,' he said. 'That's gonna be another dollar.'

'Louis, darling, would you give this sweet little boy five dollars just for me.'

The Count handed Red five dollars.

'Five dollars! Gosh, thanks, lady. I bet you're going to be the prettiest bride in the whole state.'

'When you say "bet",' said Manmountain, 'how big a bet exactly?'

'Do not bet with Lenny Manmountain, honey,' smiled Bella. 'Lenny Manmountain never lost a bet yet. Take a left, please,' she added as they reached the edge of town.

They turned down a narrow street. At the end, set back from the road, was an abandoned house, its windows shuttered and dark. Hunched over it, like a giant hippopotamus about to swallow it whole, was a vast, shadowy barn.

'Here we are!' shouted Bella. 'I think the pageboy should open the doors.'

'Wait,' said Jem. 'This isn't a church.'

'Excellent observational skills,' said the bride-to-be, patting Jem on the head as she climbed out of the car. 'I suppose that's important if you're a getaway driver.'

'But if it's not a church . . .' pressed Jem.

'. . . then it's a surprise. In we go. I am most excited. Groom first. Then our guests, Red and the Tooting family, then my bridesmaid . . .

and finally Mr Lenny Manmountain . . .'

When Jem tried to follow the others in, Bella put her hand on his chest and said, 'Stay in the car. Keep the engine running. We won't be long.'

'But . . .'

As he tried to protest, Red came running out. 'Rope,' he said. 'The big guy says he needs some rope.'

'Why would you need rope for a wedding?'

'Does the phrase "tying the knot" mean nothing to you?' snapped Bella. 'Get some rope.'

'We don't have any rope. Just that pile of prehistoric spider's web . . .'

Red picked up the hunk of spider's web and ran back inside. One second later, he was outside again, wiping strands of spider's web from his hands.

'Violin,' he said.

'On the back seat of the car.'

'You know, no one mentioned all this running and fetching. It could cost you another dollar.'

'Just hurry it up, kid. Some of us are waiting to get married.'

Red dashed back inside the barn.

There was a flash of flame.

A burst of gunfire.

A yell. A scream.

Manmountain strode out of the barn, followed

by Red. He slammed the door behind them. 'That concludes our business for today,' he said. 'OK, Diamonds, move it.'

'What?' screamed Jem. 'What did you just do to my family?'

Manmountain reassured Jem that his family wasn't dead. 'At least, not yet they ain't. If you want to keep it that way, drive and drive fast.'

'But what have you done with them?'

'Kid, you're the getaway driver, not a talk-show host,' snarled Manmountain. 'Just drive.'

'I won't!' yelled Jem. 'You can't make me!'

'Now we both know that that isn't true,' smiled Bella Sposa.

'Say what you like,' said Jem. 'Chitty Chitty Bang Bang won't go anywhere without the Tooting family. She probably won't even start without them.'

'Like a bet on that?' asked Manmountain.

'He hasn't lost a bet yet,' warned Bella Sposa.

'I bet my life on it.'

Manmountain cranked the engine, then leaned into the car and pressed the starter motor. Chitty started first time.

'You lose,' smiled Manmountain. 'Now drive. We'll sort out the life you betted later.'

5

As soon as the Tootings and the Count were inside the barn, Manmountain had opened the violin case Red had brought him and said, 'Put your hands in the air.'

'Oh, marvellous! Another new dance craze!' cried the Count.

'This is not a dance. This is a stick-up. Put your hands up or I'll shoot.' Manmountain opened his violin case, took out a machine gun and fired into the air, frightening a lot of pigeons and making jagged holes in the roof of the barn.

'Here, kid,' said Manmountain, throwing Red the ball of prehistoric spider's web. 'Help me tie these good folks to that wooden pole there.'

'OK, but it'll cost you. Another dollar at least,' said Red.

The barn smelt of damp and hay. The only light came from the handful of sunbeams that stabbed through the holes in the roof made by Manmountain's machine gun.

'Weddings are so much more complicated than I imagined,' said the Count. 'I honestly thought there was going to be a bit of confetti, some prayers and a cake. This is masses more interesting. What happens next?'

'Hmm,' said Dad. 'I'm trying to think.'

Dad felt something tugging at his wrist. He tried to look around but he was tied so tightly all he could see when he moved his head was Lucy's butterfly-infested hair.

'I suppose she did say we would be tying the knot,' said the Count.

Now Lucy felt a tug on her arm. At first she thought it was her phone vibrating but then Dad said, 'What is that tugging?' so he could feel it too. He tugged back. Something was on the other end of the spider's web.

'Little Harry?' said Lucy. 'Where is he?'

'Little Harry?' called Mum.

A happy little voice answered from the dark. 'Sticky!' it said.

Yes! Manmountain had forgotten to tie up Little

Harry. But the toddler had somehow managed to get himself stuck to the loose end of the spider's web. Gently Dad tugged at the rope, pulling Little Harry nearer and nearer.

'Sticky!' he cried.

'Yes, Little Harry, sticky,' said Dad. If he could just get him near enough then his youngest son might be able to help them free themselves.

'Bang! Bang!' cried Little Harry.

'Yes, Chitty Chitty Bang Bang is gone,' said Dad. 'But we'll get her back . . .'

'Bang! Bang!' insisted Little Harry.

If Jem had been there he might have figured out exactly what Little Harry was trying to say. But he wasn't, so everyone just asssumed that he was talking about Chitty Chitty Bang Bang.

That's why everyone was so surprised when Little Harry toddled out of the shadows saying, 'Bang! Bang!' and carrying a machine gun.

'Now, Little Harry,' said Mum, with all the quiet and calm she could muster, 'put the gun down. Put it down very gently.'

'Bang! Bang!' said Little Harry.

'Exactly,' said Mum. 'We'll all go bang-bang and we don't want that, do we?'

'Please put it down, Little Harry,' begged Dad.

'Nothing to worry about, everyone,' said the Count. 'I'm wearing my lucky cufflinks. Nothing ever goes wrong when I'm wearing my luck—'

Little Harry had dropped the machine gun. The moment it hit the floor it erupted, spraying bullets, thunder, noise and smoke all around the barn. Wood splintered above their heads. Earth flew up from the floor. Wisps of hay swarmed through the air.

When the shooting stopped, the air was full of smoke and gunpowder and Little Harry was sitting on the floor with a big grin on his fat little face. He clapped his hands and said, 'Bang! Bang!' one more time.

'No one hurt?' said the Count. 'Thank you, lucky cufflinks. Oh I say! What was that?'

The huge wooden pole to which Manmountain had tied them creaked, swayed, creaked again. It had been cut in half by a rain of bullets. Now it was falling over.

'If we all lean the same way,' said Dad, straining. 'Yes, that's it . . .' They guided the pole to the ground and with a bit of wriggling and some lifting they were able to slide the spider's web rope off the end of it and free themselves.

'That's better,' smiled the Count, dusting himself down. 'Now where can my bride have possibly got to?'

'This is just a guess,' said Lucy, 'but Manmountain is a professional gambler. You are favourite to win the Greatest Motor Race in the World, which is just about to start. Manmountain has kidnapped you and left you here so that you can't enter the race. Meanwhile he's bet on another car to win . . .'

'Of course!' cried Mum. 'Chitty Chitty Bang Bang! He's bet a fortune on her and, since the Count can't enter, he's bound to win.'

'But who would drive her?' asked the Count.

'Isn't it obvious? The best getaway driver in New York. Jem.'

'My poor Jem!' sobbed Mum. 'He'll be killed. Dad! Stop them.'

'How can I stop them?' said Dad. 'They've got a car that can fly and sail and travel in time.'

'The finest getaway car in the world.'

'What can I do? What can any of us do?' sighed Dad.

Bang! The barn doors burst into splinters.

Bang! A bomb of sunlight exploded around them.

'Chitty!' stuttered an engine. A massive machine, gleaming with chrome and smelling of petrol, rammed through the shattered door.

'Chitty!' It said again as it screeched to a halt in front of them.

'Sorry if I frightened you,' said Jem, putting on the handbrake. 'Going a bit faster than I meant to.'

'What happened?' said Mum.

'Well, Count Louis is the favourite for the Greatest Motor Race on Earth, which is just about to start. Lenny Manmountain thought that if he captured the Count and held him prisoner here on Long Island, he could bet on Chitty Chitty Bang Bang to win instead. He was bound to win with me driving because I'm the greatest getaway driver in New York. Then he would pick up the prize and win a huge bet.'

'That's exactly what Lucy said,' gasped the Count, looking at her with disbelief. 'How did you know?'

'It was obvious,' blushed Lucy.

'How did you get away from them?' asked Mum.

'It wasn't me,' admitted Jem. 'It was Chitty. About a mile from here, there's a hill. She raced up it and just as we were coming to the summit, this little blue light started flashing on the dashboard. I know better than to ignore Chitty so I pressed it. Turned out to be an ejector seat. Just as we hit the top of the hill, the back seat flipped up and threw the two of them into the air. I saw them come down in a field. Then Chitty turned around and came to the rescue.'

'Good old Chitty,' said Mum, patting her bonnet.

'Let's see if we can get this seat back into place,' said Dad. The back seat had flipped over on to Chitty's boot when it ejected Bella and Lenny.

They wound its muscular springs back into place and pulled it up again. As soon it started to move, they realized that something, or someone, was trapped underneath.

'Am I dead?' came a boy's voice as a mop of red hair flashed in the bullet-hole sunlight.

'No, no, Red,' soothed Lucy. 'You're not dead. You're just wearing ridiculous clothes.'

'You got wedged under the seat when Chitty ejected Bella and Lenny,' said Jem. 'Chitty must like you or she would've ejected you too.'

'Well,' said Lucy. 'At least we can change out of these silly outfits.'

'Let me get this clear,' said the Count. 'Am I married yet?'

'No.'

'Gosh, weddings take a dashed long time, what with all the tying people up, and firing machine guns and so on. Or

am I being impatient just because I'm excited?'

'No,' agreed Mum, 'it *is* more complicated than most weddings.'

The Tootings looked at each other uncomfortably. None of them wanted to explain that a bride-to-be who ties you up in a barn, fires a machine gun at you and then drives off in your car is probably not the bride-to-be for you.

'I have half a mind,' said the Count, 'to skip the whole thing and go straight to the Prix d'Esmerelda's Birthday Cake.'

'Great idea!' said Dad, a bit too quickly. 'Isn't that a great idea, everyone?'

'Of course, I could never do it really,' sighed the Count. 'It would disappoint the lady, and a gentleman never disappoints a lady.'

'Speaking as a girl . . .' said Lucy.

'Which is exactly what you are,' said the Count.

'. . . I think she won't be disappointed.'

'Gosh, that would be terrific. But I say, why wouldn't she be disappointed?'

'Hard to explain. It's a girl thing. Girls change their minds a lot.'

'I see. So . . .'

'Go and race. It's what you're good at. Chitty will get you to the starting line, won't you, Chitty?'

'Ga gooo ga!' sang Chitty.

6

The first person ever to own a car in America was a young man from New York by the name of D. Runyon Van Mellon. The car was a Renault Voiturette, which he had imported from Paris. The day it rolled off the boat, he had a quick read of the manual, cranked up the engine and set out for his mother's house in Connecticut. It was her birthday and the car was going to be her birthday present. D. Runyon Van Mellon hadn't read the bit in the manual about filling up the tank, so he just kept going until he ran out of petrol. The people in the small town where he came to a stop had never seen a car before. They were excited and generous. Some of them had their photo taken with it, while others went to fetch petrol. But when D. Runyon asked for directions to Connecticut they had no idea how to get there. D. Runyon made a guess and carried on until he ran out of petrol again. In that town, people had never even heard of Connecticut. Anxious not to miss his mother's birthday, D. Runyon drove on and on, increasingly worried because whenever he stopped to fill up with petrol, nobody seemed to have heard of Connecticut. Even so, it was still quite a shock when the sun came up one morning on sand and cacti and men on horses driving cattle through clouds of dust. Hungry, thirsty and very much in need of a change of underwear, D. Runyon Van Mellon had arrived in New Mexico. Three and a half thousand miles off target.

D. Runyon was a proud young man. He pretended to have done it all on purpose, took a right and headed back towards New York. It made him the first man to drive completely round the United States – an amazing feat of endurance. Anyone who cared to trace his circular tour on a map could see it was the shape of a gigantic birthday cake – a cake the size of America – which he had driven in honour of his mother. So the Greatest Automobile Race in the World – the Prix d'Esmerelda's Birthday Cake – was born. It took place on the birthday of Mrs Esmerelda Van Mellon. Every year, thousands gathered to watch the start. A brass band blew a bright blast and, in an earthquake of engines, the Esmerelda Van Mellon Birthday Trophy – the longest, toughest, most dangerous, noisiest, most polluting motor race the world has ever seen – got under way.

It was always a magical and amazing day.

The Tootings missed it.

Due to the morning's kidnapping and carjacking activities, they missed the start of the race and had to chug slowly up to the field through crowds of people who were heading happily home.

'Better luck next year,' said the race steward, rolling up his chequered flag and putting it back in his chequered-flag box.

'Oh, dash it all,' sighed the Count.

'Nice meeting you, Count,' said Dad. 'Sorry about the wedding. And the race.'

'Shall we have a group photo?' said Lucy, taking out her jelly-baby phone. 'Just for the record. Oh!'

The 'oh!' was because she found that she had a voicemail message. The Tootings all gathered round to listen to it. It began with a blast of music and laughter. Then they heard Nanny shouting over the racket: *'Hey! Tootings! Your neighbours are such fun! Poor Tiny Jack needed someone to play with so I invited a few people round and guess what?! The whole street came! Tiny Jack says it's his favourite party ever. Come back soon. It makes me sad that you're missing all the fun! I suppose you're all tied up.'*

'Those people,' wailed Lucy, 'are having a party in our house!'

'To the car, everyone,' said Dad. 'We're going home right now.'

'I thought we were going to 1966 first,' said Jem. 'We won't be able to defeat Tiny Jack on our own. If we go back on our own he might get Chitty off us. We have to get the Potts to help us first.'

'Whatever we're doing,' said Mum, 'we need to start. I want those people out of my house.'

But when they went to get back into Chitty, the Count was sitting in the driving seat. 'I don't suppose I could take her for one last spin? I *have* missed the old girl.'

'Not really,' said Jem. 'We're in the middle of trying to save the world from an evil supervillain.'

'Jem!' snapped Mum. 'After the Count has been so nice – taking us to parties, inviting us to his wedding – it's the least we can do. Get in, everyone.'

'But you said . . .' objected Jem, as they settled into their seats and Dad cranked the engine.

'A lap of the park can't do any harm,' he

said incorrectly, as he clambered aboard. Very, very incorrectly.

The moment the Count touched the starter, Chitty's exhaust backfired twice – Bang! Bang! – like an artillery salute. All over the meadow people shrieked and ducked. 'Chitty-chitty-chitty-chitty,' muttered her engine. The Count let slip the handbrake. She leaped forward, bouncing down the cinder track, throwing up dust, belching smoke, racing after the other cars.

'Count, it's been an honour and a pleasure,' yelled Dad. 'But if you could just turn her round . . .'

'The wheel won't turn. Also the accelerator seems to keep – well – accelerating.'

Dad watched in horror as the needle on the speedometer crept towards a hundred miles an hour. A hundred and five. A hundred and ten. Fifteen. Twenty. Twenty-five . . . every rivet in Chitty's body rattled. Her engine whined. Her passengers screamed.

'We're never going to make it!' yelled Mum as they hurtled towards a sharp left bend.

For the briefest moment Chitty slowed down into the bend, but then she powered out of it at a hundred and thirty . . .

'She always was good on the corners,' yelled the Count.

'That's a comfort,' said Lucy, 'because there's another one right ahead.'

'What?' gasped the Count.

'The road is bending back on itself as it descends an incredibly steep hill . . .'

'I see, but . . .'

It was too late. Chitty smashed through the fence that marked the side of the road, and leaped into the air.

Jem was almost relieved when he felt Chitty leave the ground. Surely now her wings will open, he thought, and we'll fly gently and happily above the trouble. But no . . . There was a terrifying crunch as Chitty smacked into the rocky ground, barged through undergrowth, skittered over scree.

Below them they could see the next bend in the road and a convoy of cars speeding along the highway, jostling and dodging around each other.

'That's the race!' yelled the Count triumphantly. 'We're in with a chance after all.'

'No, we're not in with a chance,' said Dad. 'Because we're not in the race. The word today is *stop the car, we have a world to save!*'

'Are you sure that's all one word, old sport? It sounds like quite a mouthful to me.'

Chitty swung on to the highway.

*

Motor racing is a dangerous and demanding sport. The great skill of it is to get your car into a good position, wait for the driver in front to take a corner a little bit wide, or come out of a turn just a bit too slowly, or fail to accelerate decisively enough down the straight, then grab your opportunity and roar into the lead. Most drivers like to do it with a mixture of cunning and courage. Chitty Chitty Bang Bang didn't bother with the courage or the cunning. She preferred force and fear. She didn't slide through the gap. She blazed up to the bumper, headlights glaring, klaxon blaring. She shunted the cars in front of her, barged the cars alongside her, shovelled smoke at anyone who tried to sneak up behind. Drivers slowed down, pulled over, let her pass, afraid that she was some terrible mechanical demon.

Soon there was just one single car ahead of them. Unlike the other cars, it made hardly any noise. No clouds of smoke came shovelling from its exhaust. Quick, quiet and creamy white, it threaded through the chicanes, and slid round bends like a high-speed ghost.

'We'll never catch that,' said Dad. 'Unless it wants to be caught.'

It seemed that the ghost car did want to be caught.

They squealed around a tight bend and saw

a long stretch of flat, straight road rolling out in front of them. There was the white car – half a mile ahead, dawdling along, as if it were waiting for them to catch up.

'Tinkety-tonk!' whooped the Count. 'They want a proper race!'

He crunched down on the accelerator. Chitty shot forward and was sliding into place right alongside the ghost car. She really was a beauty – streamlined and glossy. Her silvery wheels rolled effortlessly over the rough road. Her windscreen gleamed. Her fenders shone. Her engine purred. At the wheel was the composed and immaculate figure of Crackitt the butler.

'Great gallons of gasoline!' exclaimed the Count. 'That's Chitty the Second! That's my new car! Crackitt! What are you doing?'

Crackitt gave the Count a deep, respectful nod.

'It's no good. He can't hear me over Chitty's engine.'

Crackitt, however, had thought of that. He produced a brilliantly shiny silver megaphone and addressed the Count through it. 'When you were late for the start, m'lord,' he boomed, 'I took the liberty of driving the car myself. I formed the view that a man of your brilliance and resource would very soon catch up with me, even if I was doing a hundred and forty-five miles per hour. And that you would prefer to win the race if at all possible. If you're ready, sir, I'll leave the rest of the race to you.'

Crackitt opened the door of Chitty the Second and shuffled over into the passenger seat. What he did not do was slow down. Both cars were moving at something close to a hundred miles per hour.

This didn't seem to bother the Count. He climbed right over Dad, and opened Chitty's door. With no one in charge of her, Chitty careened all over the road, until Dad dived into the driver's seat and grabbed her wheel. The Count stood for a moment with a foot on both cars. 'So you'll be doing the race with me, Crackitt. That'll be cosy.'

'I'm afraid not, sir. I have ironing and dusting to do at the house. I made arrangements for my return there, the moment you were available.' He nodded down the road. Speeding towards them, just a few feet above the ground, was a small yellow biplane.

'Propellers!' yelled Jem. 'Duck!' The plane's propellers – like the blades of a giant, unseeing food blender – were heading straight for them. 'They're going to dice us like human pesto. And car pesto. Car-and-human pesto . . .'

'Louis!' yelled Lucy. 'Duck!'

'What? Oh! Ah. Excellent suggestion,' said the Count, bobbing his head just as the plane thundered over it.

'If you'll excuse me, sir,' yelled Crackitt. The butler leaped up and grabbed the plane's axle as it soared away with him into the wild blue sky.

'*Au revoir*, Crackitt!'

'Indeed, sir, I'll have the kettle on for when you return.'

The Count was still standing with one foot on each car but now that there was no one in Chitty the Second's driving seat, this position was becoming more difficult to maintain. He clambered into the other car, then, just as he was sitting down, looked back at the Original and Best Chitty Chitty Bang Bang and at Lucy.

'What ho!' he called. 'Care for a spin?'

'Oh!' said Lucy. 'Yes. Please.'

'No, Lucy,' warned Dad as Lucy steadied herself at Chitty's door, ready to leap into the other car. 'What have we told you about jumping back and forth between speeding racing cars?'

'Nothing,' said Lucy. 'The subject never really came up.'

The Count held out his hand to her. She stood there with the freezing wind blasting through her hair, about to make the leap from one car to the other. She tingled with a sense of how fantastically, brilliantly wonderful life had been since Chitty came along. Before Chitty came she would go for weeks – years even – without seeing giant squid, or rampaging dinosaurs, or a gun-crazy gambler dressed as a bride. The reason Dad had never given her advice about leaping between speeding racing cars is that it wasn't something she'd ever had to do. He'd given her advice on not squeezing the toothpaste in the middle, and making her bed before leaving for school, because until Chitty came along brushing her teeth might well be the highlight of her day. Now here she was speeding along, about to jump into the arms of the dashing young Count and roar off into the lead in the world-famous Prix d'Esmerelda's Birthday Cake! She was suddenly filled with love for Chitty, for Dad, for Jem, Mum and Little Harry, for taking her on this fantastic adventure.

'Jump, Lucy! Don't be scared!' called the Count.

What was he on about? She wasn't scared!

'Come and see how the new, improved Chitty runs!'

Those were probably not the best words to use around the Original and Best Chitty Chitty Bang Bang. The roar of her engine dropped to a growl. 'Bang!' went her exhaust and, inevitably, 'Bang!' again. These bangs were so loud that the whole car shuddered and Lucy was flung into the back seat of the Original and Best Chitty, which then thundered past her 'new, improved' version, and swung in front, waggling her triumphant fender from side to side, honking her defiant horn, and showering the immaculate white car with dust and fumes.

'Whoa! We're going to win this race!' shrieked Red.

But the new, improved Chitty slid easily past the Original and Best, with barely a sound. She did not waggle her triumphant fender or honk her defiant horn. She just got smaller and smaller as she sped into the distance. Chitty slowed down, as if she had given up hope, as if she didn't care any more.

'Hey!' yelled Jem. 'What're you doing? Don't touch those!'

Red had clambered over into the front seat. He was fiddling with Chitty's dials and buttons. 'Manmountain gave me twenty-five dollars to make sure the Count doesn't win this race. We gotta beat him. Come on. I thought you were a great driver. Give me a hand here. Is this the thing to make it go faster?'

'Don't touch that!' warned Dad, trying to shove Red aside.

'Really don't touch it!' shouted Jem, trying to pull Red away.

As they struggled, Chitty hit the verge. Then she hit the other verge.

'Don't touch that handle. Please don't touch that—'

It was too late. Red had grabbed the Chronojuster and was jerking it up and down in its slot when Chitty hit the bend and somersaulted into the air with every Tooting screaming.

7

Where before they could hear nothing but the roar of Chitty's engine, now they could hear a skylark stitching its song into the blue afternoon.

Where before the air had been blowing round their heads like an ice-cold, turbo-charged hairdryer, now it was gently caressing their cheeks.

Where before the sky had been high over their heads, now the sky was nowhere in sight and what looked like the ground was hundreds of feet below them.

'Hey! What's the big idea?' snapped Red, who was holding on to the steering wheel, with his legs somehow dangling in the air.

'It seems,' said Lucy, who – like all the Tootings – was sensibly wearing her seat belt, 'that we are sitting completely still, upside down in mid-air, breaking all the laws of physics.'

'I never broke no law!' yelled Red. 'You can't put that on me. Let me go!'

'Go when you like,' shrugged Lucy. 'All you have to do is let go of the wheel. But unless you've got a parachute, you'll probably find yourself splattered like jam a thousand feet below.'

This is what had happened. When Chitty somersaulted off the road and then over a cliff, Dad had pressed on her brakes. Most brakes don't work in mid-air. Slam on an aeroplane's brakes, for

instance, and it will drop like a stone and smash into the ground. Chitty's brakes were different. When Dad pressed on them, she stopped and parked elegantly in the middle of the air.

'Shall we go back down then?' said Mum.

'Not sure,' muttered Dad.

'Not sure what?'

'My foot is still on the brake. What if I take it off the brake and she starts falling? What if I take the handbrake off and the wings go in? What if—'

'Honestly,' said Mum, 'I think we should just trust Chitty.'

Honestly, thought Jem, I'm not sure we can.

'We can't stay up here forever,' said Mum and reached across Dad for the handbrake.

'Wait!' said Dad. 'Just let me think.'

'Better not to,' said Mum. 'Whenever you think, it all goes wrong.'

She slipped the handbrake. Chitty turned an elegant loop in the air, came the right way up, spread her wings and began a long, lazy glide towards the ground. Of course, when her engine started up, so did the Chronojuster and once again they felt the bubbles of time breezing through their bodies.

'What's going on!? It tickles,' said Red, as he sank back into the safety of his seat. 'It tickles. And . . . whoa . . . what is that?!'

Far below them, as far as any of them could see, stretched a forest. Long, wispy clouds flew like banners over the vast army of trees.

'That's rainforest,' said Lucy.

'I'm setting a course for 1966,' said Dad.

'Which way would that be?' asked Lucy.

'Well . . . forwards . . . about forty years forwards.'

'We've moved in time since then,' said Lucy. 'And we don't know in which direction. Red just bashed the Chronojuster up and down. That forest could be a thousand years in the past. Or it could be in some strange future. We need to go down there and find out before we move.'

'Where would we land?' said Jem. 'There's no space.'

'Yes there is,' said Red. 'Over there. See that gap between the trees? It has to be a landing site.'

'Well spotted, Red,' said Dad, as he carefully adjusted the wing flaps and circled slowly towards the landing site.

Red shrugged. 'You live on the street, you learn to notice stuff.'

But it wasn't a landing site at all. It was a fat, brown river. One of the switches on Chitty's dashboard flashed on and off as if the car herself was reminding Dad that she couldn't just land in the water.

'Mister! We're crashing! We're going to drown!' yelled Red.

'Don't worry,' said Dad, flicking the illuminated switch.

Chitty withdrew her wheels and extended her floats. She skimmed the surface for a while, then slid on to the water like a duck landing on a pond. They chugged up a river that was so overhung with trees that they often had to duck or push them aside. Red and Jem climbed out on to Chitty's long, elegant bonnet, perching just behind Chitty's mascot – the Zborowski Lightning – and pushing the branches aside. The air was warm. Butterflies and dragonflies flashed in the shafts of dusty sunlight that filtered through the leaves.

'Maybe this is none of my business,' said Red, 'but where are we?'

'Judging by the density of the forest,' said Lucy, 'I would say Africa. Or maybe Amazonia.'

'You mean . . . we're out of state? We're not in New York any more?'

An alligator slid from the river's slippery banks into the water, speeding towards them without a ripple.

'No,' said Lucy, 'I don't think this is New York.'

'Don't worry,' said Mum, whacking the approaching alligator on the nose with her handbag. 'We'll take you home as soon as we get our bearings.'

'We gotta win that race, lady. There's twenty-five dollars riding on it.'

'Yes, yes,' said Mum. 'Meanwhile how about a game of I Spy? That usually helps pass the time on long car journeys.'

'I'm no spy, lady. I did nothing wrong.'

'I Spy is a game. You must have played it.'

Red looked completely blank.

'But you must have played it. You just look around you. Pick an object and then tell us the first letter of its name and we have to guess what it is.'

'Do I get paid if you guess right?'

'No. It's just for fun.'

Red looked blank again. It seemed like unpaid fun was a new idea to him.

'I ain't stupid, ma'am. I can give you the best shoeshine on the whole island of Manhattan. Ask anyone. Wanna know my secret? Well, it's a secret.'

'But you don't know any games? Look. If I say . . . "I spy with my little eye something beginning with P" . . . give it a try.'

'Puma!' yelled Little Harry. There really was a puma following them along the riverbank.

'Very good, Little Harry. Now you try, Red.'

'The secret of a great shoeshine is to spray water on the polish before you brush it off.'

'I spy with my little eye something beginning with P,' said Lucy.

The answer turned out to be a pangolin – a kind of armoured anteater – which was bowling along the muddy shore. Only Lucy had ever heard of it so she won and gave her turn to Red.

'Does it have to be P every time?' said Red.

'No. It can be any letter you like.'

'OK then, P it is . . . for piranhas. Just there . . .'

Lucy had been dangling her hand in the water. She pulled it out hastily now. 'You're supposed to let us guess,' she said. 'But on this occasion I'm glad you didn't.'

'Fish! Fish! Bitey fish!' yelled Little Harry, trying to reach into the water, to feed his own hand to the piranhas.

'No, Little Harry!' said Jem. He grabbed the strip of Cretaceous spider's web that was still stuck to Little Harry's wrist and yanked him back into his seat. 'That was handy,' said Jem. 'Just what you need: a sticky and unbreakable leash.'

They drifted upstream I-spying otters and capybaras, macaws and rubber trees and waterfalls. When Red asked for 'something beginning with F', no one guessed it and he said, 'Folks!'

'What?'

'People.'

'People begins with P.'

'That's why I said "folks".'

'What folks?'

'Them folks there . . .' He pointed to the left bank.

'I can't see anyone,' said Jem.

'Keep watching. See that tree? The one that hangs right over? Behind the root . . .'

Jem stared and stared. A branch twitched. There was a faint sound that could have been a whisper. 'Is there someone there?' he said.

'Ten someones,' said Red.

'All I can see is leaves.'

'When you live on the streets of New York City,' said Red, 'you learn to keep an eye out for trouble.'

8

The people who were watching Chitty pass through the trees were hunters who had lived all their lives in the rainforest. They could pass through thick undergrowth without bending a leaf. They could run without breaking a twig. They painted their bodies in thick earthy paints for camouflage. Thanks to their ancient skills they could pass, invisible and silent, through the forest. Once they'd had a look at Chitty, though, they couldn't be bothered with any of that.

When Chitty came chugging round the next bend, the Tootings found the banks lined with people. People who were not invisible or silent at all – people who were cheering and waving. Families leaped into canoes to follow the great car up the river. A group of young men paddled ahead of them as if leading the way. By the time she hit the next bend, she was the flagship of a navy of excited canoes.

None of this was much of a surprise to the Tootings. Wherever they had gone in the world, people (as opposed to dinosaurs) had been thrilled to see Chitty – her gorgeous green paintwork, her gleaming exhausts. After all, Chitty was a work of art and if you drive a work of art, people stop and look.

Beyond the bend, the river widened into a lagoon whose gently sloping gravel shores were crowded with more people, waving and pointing. Suddenly all the men on the bank raised their arms shook their feathered bracelets and yelled, 'Chitty! Chitty!'

All the women raised their bows and arrows and replied, 'Bang! Bang!'

They did it again.

'Chitty! Chitty!'

'Bang! Bang!'

One little girl said, 'Bang!' a bit after everyone else and everyone laughed happily at her mistake. Then they started to sing a song about Chitty Chitty Bang Bang.

'These people have a song about our car,' said Lucy. 'Doesn't that worry you?'

'They're just very excited to see us,' said Mum. 'Maybe they don't get many visitors. Can you understand the words, Lucy?'

'They must be speaking one of the lost languages of Amazonia, which were all wiped out when the conquistadores arrived in the sixteenth century. So . . . no.'

When Dad drove Chitty up on to the riverbank, children clambered on to her running-boards, her bonnet and her bumpers. Teenage girls ran up and honked her horn. They greeted her like an old friend. Men came running from the trees with lianas and ropes and fastened them to Chitty's fenders and pulled her through the town, singing and clapping 'Bang! Bang!' and 'Chitty! Chitty!' as they went. And what a town it was. The houses were all raised on wooden stilts ('for when the river rises,' said Lucy). Children and strange, chickeny birds played in and out of the space between the stilts. All the houses were different – some had round windows, some had paintings on the outside, some had buckets of flowers hanging from every corner, some were covered in carvings – but none of them looked poor and none of them looked grand. Everyone was dressed differently but everyone's clothes were bright and new.

In the middle of the town was a market. There

were piles of brilliantly coloured fruit and fat vegetables, and troughs full of fish. Unlike the markets at home, people stopped and took things from the piles.

'Hey!' whispered Red. 'Those people are just taking stuff and not paying for it.'

'This seems to be a society that doesn't use money,' said Lucy.

'You mean they're all robbers?' asked Red.

'No. They just don't need money. They share what they have.'

'Wow,' said Red. 'We've got to get out of here.'

'I think it's rather sweet,' said Mum.

'Sure. Until they want us to share Chitty Chitty Bang Bang.'

At the far end of the square was a house that looked completely different from all the others. It was not on stilts or covered in beautiful carvings. It sat square on the ground. Its garden was surrounded by a fence. There was a path leading to the front door. It had a pointy roof and four windows – though there was no glass in them. Where all the other houses had a platform you could climb on to, this one had a front door with a knocker on it. In other words it was exactly the kind of house you might see in Basildon. Except it was in the middle of the jungle. Next to the house was a small, flat-roofed garage with an up-

and-over door which suddenly opened as they got nearer. Two big women strode out to meet them. Not big like your mum's friend who's too big for her dress, but big like boxers, or basketball players, or big, beautiful statues. Their hair flowed over their shoulders like shiny black waterfalls, decorated with clusters of jewel-bright feathers. The two women were so alike that at first Jem thought they weren't two women at all, but one woman twice. Their faces were identical. Their hair was identical. They were wearing identical clothes and identical feathers. When one of them raised her finger in the air, the other did the same. When one of them spoke it was as though someone had pressed the mute button on the whole forest. Everything was quiet and listening, even the insects. This is what she said.

'Where on earth have you been? We've been waiting literally ages, haven't we, Imogen?'

'We really, really have, Eliza. We've been waiting for generations.'

'Absolutely generations.'

'You speak English?' asked Mum.

'Is that what you call it?' said Eliza. 'We call it Chitty Talk, don't we, Imogen?'

'We do, Eliza. Can I say you're all certainly super-welcome here in Manau, but Chitty is the most especially welcome.'

Imogen crouched down in front of Chitty's radiator and said, 'Chitty Chitty Bang Bang, it's soooo wonderful that you've come back to us at last.'

Eliza crouched down next to her sister. 'We always hoped to see you,' she said, patting Chitty on the fender. 'Are you going to stay with us long?'

The whole crowd held its breath, waiting for the car to reply. The Tootings looked at each other. No one wanted to be the one to say that Chitty couldn't talk.

'Cars don't talk,' said Red.

'Now that,' said Imogen, straightening up, 'is very much a disappointment.'

'How do you know her name?' asked Jem. 'Have you seen her before?'

'Seen her?' said Imogen. 'No. Heard of her? Yes. Waited for her? Double yes with bells on top.'

'Some people said she was just a story but now here she is. Real as rain and pretty as paint.'

'I always believed in Chitty but now that she's here . . . somehow I don't believe it! Can we touch her?'

'Of course.'

All the people formed an orderly queue and one by one they touched Chitty's bodywork. Some of them strewed flowers across her bonnet, or twisted blossom in between the spokes of her wheels.

'I think we're allowed to sit in her,' said Imogen. 'After all, we are the Queen.'

'By all means,' said Dad, opening Chitty's door so that the twins could climb in. 'Are you both Queens or is one of you the Queen and one of you . . . not?'

'We're both the Queen,' said Eliza.

'It takes two people to be Queen,' said Imogen.

'You can't be Queen unless there's two of you,' explained Eliza.

'I must say,' said Mum, 'I love your bracelet.'

'Really?' said Eliza. 'Then it's yours.'

'Oh, I couldn't. Really . . .'

But Eliza held out her wrist to Mum and, as she did so, her splendid bracelet separated into six bright pieces and those pieces flitted around her head. It wasn't a bracelet at all. It was a charm of tiny hummingbirds, trained to perch on her wrist or flit around her head like a living veil. Mum cooed in wonder as the hummingbirds flashed and thrummed around her.

'The garage is perfect, by the way,' said Dad.

'You like it, it's yours,' said Imogen.

'Oh no, we couldn't.'

'You like it, so it's yours,' insisted Eliza, as though she was describing a law of physics.

'Do you like the house?' asked Eliza.

The only polite thing Mum could say was 'yes,' even though she knew what was coming next . . .

'Yours,' said the twins together.

'The rule seems to be,' said Lucy, 'that if you say you like something, they give it to you.'

'Oh, I love this one's hair,' sighed Eliza.

'It's gorgeous, like gold,' swooned Imogen.

'No!' gasped Red, clamping his hands on his head. 'Don't let them take my hair!' But it seemed that all they wanted was to twiddle their fingers through his curls.

Inside the house was a long wooden table where baskets of luscious berries and shiny fruit snuggled up to sizzling slices of fish laid out on leaves the size of dinner plates. Wooden goblets brimmed with unfamiliar juices.

'I never saw this much food in all my life,' said Red.

'It's all yours,' said Eliza.

'Absolutely every crumb,' said Imogen.

'Ever since the days of our great-grandmother, we've laid a feast out here each day, ready for the return of Chitty Chitty Bang Bang. And now she has returned. This is a great day. Please, eat . . .'

'What happened to all the food on all the thousands of days we never came?' asked Lucy.

'Every night the people came and ate it all. As they ate, they thanked Chitty Chitty Bang Bang. Even though she wasn't there. The feast was her present to them.'

'Great-Grandmother's painting helped us think of her,' said Imogen.

The wall was covered by a colourful painting. It showed a gorgeous old racing car with a handsome man at the wheel, an elegant woman next to him and two pretty children in the back seats.

'She really caught Chitty perfectly,' said Imogen.

'It's a super-perfect likeness. Every screw and every rivet.'

'Every rivet and every screw.'

'Of course, the people look nothing like you.'

'No,' agreed Mum, thinking to herself, *The woman is at least two dress sizes bigger than me.*

'Definitely not,' said Dad, thinking, *I've got a lot more hair than him.*

120

'Nothing like us,' said Lucy, who thought the girl looked revoltingly girly.

'It's not us,' said Jem, flicking through the logbook. 'That is the Pott family – that's Commander Pott, the man who gave Chitty her green-striped wings.'

'Never mind,' said Imogen. 'As long as Chitty is here, that's all that matters. Great-Grandmother said Chitty Chitty Bang Bang would return, which she has.'

'And she said the car would solve all our problems. Which I'm sure she will.'

'You have problems?' asked Dad, tucking into the biggest, juiciest mango he had ever seen in his life. 'But this place seems so happy and wonderful.'

'We have heaps of problems.'

'Heaps on top of heaps.'

'And heaps underneath heaps. Life is just stress and more stress here.'

'With a break for stress.'

'That's why we love Chitty Chitty Bang Bang,' said Imogen, staring deep into Dad's eyes.

'We really, *really* love Chitty Chitty Bang Bang,' added Eliza, staring pointedly into Mum's eyes.

All at once the room was filled with an awkward silence. Mum and Dad both understood that when the twins said they loved Chitty Chitty Bang Bang, the polite thing to say was, 'OK then, she's all yours.' But how could they say that? Without Chitty to take them home, they would be trapped forever in sixteenth-century Amazonia. Because that's where they were. Mum looked at Dad. Dad looked at Mum. Parents looked at children. Everyone looked at the ground.

When they looked up, the twins and all the people of Manau had gone.

'Well, that was embarrassing,' said Lucy.

'What else could we do? We can't stay in the Amazon forever. We haven't packed for it.'

'Besides,' said Jem, 'we are actually on a mission to find the Potts and save the world from Tiny Jack.'

'That's true,' said Dad. 'But honestly you should try these mangoes first.'

'I am really hungry,' admitted Jem.

'Not surprising,' said Lucy. 'It's five centuries since supper and sixty-six million years since breakfast.'

Maybe it was because all the food was strange and new, maybe it was because it was so fresh and juicy, but while they ate, they forgot about everything else. The fish was cooked in a sauce so surprising and complicated, their brains busied themselves trying to identify the ingredients. There were fruits the size of apples with hard spiky skin that, when opened, had flesh of different colours. They were bursting with a rich, sweet, sticky juice so delicious that all the thoughts that Jem might have been thinking – about how to save the world from Tiny Jack, how to repay the kindness of the twin Queens – dissolved.

'Gone!' said Little Harry. 'Gone, gone, gone.'

'No,' soothed Mum, 'there's plenty of everything left, Little Harry, take as much as you like.'

'Gone,' said Little Harry again.

'Maybe he wants a drink,' said Dad, picking up a steaming jug brimming with a dark, frothing liquid. He poured some for each of them. It looked a bit like coffee but tasted like electricity and lit up your brain. Jem wondered what it was. Lucy said she believed it was chocolate.

'It doesn't taste a bit like chocolate.'

'In the past, the people here didn't make chocolate into sugary bars, they made it into a hot spicy drink that was supposed to wake your brain up.'

It must have woken Jem's brain because next time Little Harry said 'Gone', he remembered with a sudden clarity that Little Harry is always right. If Little Harry said something was gone, then something was gone. Jem looked around the table, to see what it might be. It was Red. Red had disappeared.

As soon as he got outside, Jem heard a frantic rattling noise coming from the garage door. Red was trying to tug it open.

'Red,' said Jem. 'It doesn't work like that. You pull it upwards and it kind of slides open. Here, I'll show you.' But as he took hold of the handle, he thought, Why is Red trying to open the garage? So he said, 'Red, why are you trying to open the garage?'

'Gonna take this car and win that race,' announced Red with a shrug. 'Lenny Manmountain said he'd give me twenty-five dollars to make sure Count Zborowski doesn't win the race. So I'm going to go out there and win it myself. You can't stop me.'

'Actually, I can stop you. You don't even know how to open the garage door.'

'Come on, help me out here. Twenty-five dollars is riding on this!'

'You were really going to run off and abandon my whole family in the jungle for just twenty-five dollars?'

'What do you mean, *just* twenty-five dollars? Twenty-five dollars is a fortune. Do you know what I could do with twenty-five dollars?'

'Look around you. These people live in this amazing place and eat amazing food and they don't have money at all.'

'I *am* looking around,' said Red, 'and I am forced to conclude that this is not New York.'

'I know this is hard to understand, but in our time, which is your future, the entire world is being threatened by a super-rich supervillain called Tiny Jack and his evil Nanny. Only Chitty Chitty Bang Bang can save the world. Without her, everything is lost. That's what the Tooting family is doing here – we are on a mission to save the world. Do you think Dad would let twenty-five dollars get in the way of that?'

'What about thirty dollars?'

'No, I think he'd ask you to think about something more important, such as saving the world.'

'What about twenty-nine dollars? Oh!'

He said 'Oh!' because all the time he had been talking to Jem, he had been fiddling with the handle of the garage door and now, quite suddenly, the door opened, sliding smoothly upward to reveal a cool, dark space lit by the busy, flickering glow of ten thousand fireflies.

'Wow,' said Jem.

'I got to admit,' said Red, 'that is pretty. Hey, do you reckon if I took a few jars of those little bugs home I could get cash for them?'

Jem said nothing. He wasn't looking at the fireflies. He was looking at the empty space in the middle of the garage. The space where the car should go. If there was a car.

Chitty had disappeared.

'I knew it,' said Red. 'They've been and gone and shared Chitty Chitty Bang Bang.'

9

'The first thing we need to do,' said Dad, 'is ask the neighbours if they saw or heard anything suspicious, then we'll call the police.'

'I'm not sure that early Amazonian societies had police forces,' said Lucy. 'Or phones.'

'Let's ask the Queen then. Go straight to the top.'

A full moon hung above the square, silvering every corner of the town with its ghostly rays as they set out to look for the Queen. By that light they could see that it wasn't just Chitty Chitty Bang Bang that was missing.

It was everyone.

In all the village there was not a flicker of light, not a whisper of conversation, not a single snore. The entire place was deserted.

'Marooned on the shores of the Amazon with no means of escape,' said Mum. 'What fun!'

'I don't think Chitty has marooned us,' said Jem. 'I think she's brought us here for a reason. Look.' He showed them Chitty's logbook. The last place that the Pott family visited was Venezuela. 'That's where we are. In 1966, they came here and after that, they disappeared. This is the last place they were ever seen. The painting of them in the house could be the last ever picture of them.'

'So the Pott family came here and suffered a terrible and mysterious fate. And now we are facing the same unspeakable doom.'

'What exactly was the unspeakable doom?' asked Dad.

'I can't say,' said Lucy, 'because it was unspeakable.'

'No,' said Jem. 'Chitty knows we need the Potts. She's brought us here so we can find them.'

'Not only can't we find them, said Dad, 'we can't find Chitty.'

'It's strange,' mused Mum. 'The Queen seemed like such nice girls. You don't think this could just be some giant game of hide-and-seek?'

Red had never heard of hide-and-seek and Lucy had to explain the rules to him. 'Can you play it for money?' he said. 'Can we play it now?'

'Maybe we should wait till morning,' said Jem. 'It must be dangerous playing hide-and-seek in a forest in the dark.'

'First clue!' yelled Red, running to a spot where a trail of deep, muddy ruts that could only have been made by a pair of wheels led into the forest. 'The only wheels round here are on your automobile.' He put back his head and yelled, 'Coming! Ready or not!' and plunged into the jungle.

Following a jungle path is very different from sailing up a jungle river. On a jungle river you have space to look around. You can see where you're going and where you have been. On the jungle floor the trees crowd together so closely that every few paces you have to change direction, squeeze through a gap, clamber over a stump, wriggle round a knot of bushes. When you look back, there's nothing to see but a confusion of trunks and branches smothering the floor.

'How could they possibly have got Chitty through here?' asked Lucy.

'They did it, though,' said Red. 'Look. We got tracks here. Here. And here. Could be they can spot paths that we can't. Come on.'

Red plunged happily in and out of the shadows.

The others tried to keep up but he vanished from view.

'Dinner!' shouted Little Harry.

'Oh, Little Harry, we've only just eaten,' scolded Mum.

'Dinner!'

'Not now, Little Harry. We're looking for Red.'

'Dinner!'

Only Jem noticed that Little Harry was pointing at something dangling from an overhanging branch. At first it was hard to figure out what the something was. It seemed as though part of the branch had been decorated with a colourful mosaic of tiny tiles, with an arm sticking out of the side. It was only after he'd looked at it from several different angles that Jem figured out what it was. Little Harry was right, of course. It was dinner. But it wasn't a little boy eating dinner. It was a little boy *being* dinner. A gigantic anaconda had trapped Red in its coils and wrapped itself around him.

'Mum!' gasped Jem.

Red's arm was waving frantically so he must still be alive in there, somewhere among the glistening yards of hungry snake muscle.

'Hey!' yelled Mum. 'Stop that right now!'

When Mum did her Furious Mum Yell at Lucy or Jem, they always dropped what they were doing

immediately. It didn't have the same effect on the anaconda. Possibly because snakes are deaf. Mum, however, was not used to being ignored. It gave her an amazing burst of strength. She leaped forward, grabbed the back end of the snake and swung from it with all her weight.

'Careful, dearest,' said Dad.

Mum's mighty swing brought snake and branch crashing down. The moment it hit the ground, it uncoiled and Red's head popped out.

'Help!' he wheezed.

'Never fear,' said Mum. The snake was already tightening its grip again but Mum had Red by the neck and was pulling him out from between the narrowing coils. She managed to get him almost clear when the snake rolled its eyes as though concentrating really hard, opened its mouth wider than you could ever have imagined possible and swallowed Red up to his knees.

'Is this part of the game?' gasped Red. 'Because if it is, can we stop playing now? I really don't like it.'

Mum turned to Dad. 'I'll hold on to Red,' she said, 'you wrench the anaconda's jaws open.'

'My anaconda-fighting skills are limited,' said Dad, 'but the word today is *don't worry, Red. Tootings to the rescue.*' Dad bravely tucked his hands in the anaconda's jaw and pulled it wider than ever. By now Red was thoroughly lubricated with snake spit, so he slid out easily when Mum pulled on him.

'Thanks, ma'am, you saved my life,' breathed Red as Mum wiped off the snake spit with a banana leaf. 'Does that mean I have to give you money?'

'No, Red, don't be silly,' smiled Mum.

'Help!' yelled Dad. No sooner had the snake lost its grip on Red than it had whipped its tail around Dad's waist and begun to squeeze. 'Help! Help!'

'Help him, Mum!' pleaded Jem.

'He's just teasing,' smiled Mum. 'Of course your Dad knows how to escape from a hungry anaconda. Hasn't he escaped from dinosaurs and gangsters already today?'

'Actually I really do need help,' wheezed Dad, turning slightly blue.

'Your father knows how to escape from every difficult situation. He knows that all you have to do if you're attacked by a boa constrictor or an anaconda is make yourself as big as possible – by holding your breath or sticking your elbows out – and then suddenly make yourself as small as possible by breathing out and tucking your elbows in. Then the snake loses its grip and you can just wriggle out. That's it. See? He's done it. He was teasing you.'

Dad stood for a while, with one arm held in the air, saying, 'I'm fine. Absolutely fine,' over and over while trying to get his breath. 'I really was teasing you.'

'What did I tell you,' smiled Mum. 'Tease. Your father is a hero. He wouldn't let a snake defeat or even delay him. And now he's going to find Chitty for us.'

Great spears of early-morning sunlight were stabbing through the branches. Butterflies with wings like sheets of wrapping paper unfolded themselves. The creaking of insects rolled across the forest floor like a wave. Now that it was daylight they could see clearly that there was no path. Nothing to follow. No reason to go this way or that.

'This is probably that unspeakable fate you were talking about, Lucy,' said Mum.

'Yes, the Pott family probably wandered

aimlessly in the endless jungle, maddened by insects, weakened by thirst and fever and finally eaten by snakes. Maybe their bones were in the stomach of the very snake that tried to eat Red.'

'Ga gooo ga!'

'What was that?'

'Ga gooo ga!'

'Chitty Chitty Bang Bang!' said Little Harry – right as usual.

'It's coming from somewhere high up.'

They could see now that one path slanted steeply upward, through the trees, towards the top of a hill. As they slogged up it, the sounds around them changed. The forest buzzed with the noise of insects but as the path wound higher, the buzz turned to the chiming of birdsong. Higher still, the birdsong was drowned out by the booming of frogs and the natter of monkeys. Suddenly they could see air through the branches and for the first time realized how big the forest was. Clouds of leaves rolled by below like a separate green sky. There was even a low, constant roar, like the waves of the sea.

'Is that a motorway?' said Jem.

'It can't be.'

'But what could it be?'

They climbed onward. All of them were thinking the same thoughts: What if this is the wrong way? What if we get lost? How could they possibly have got Chitty up here?

'Look!' yelled Red, pointing to a long, snake-like object glinting in the mud. 'Another snake! Mrs Tooting! Help me!'

'That's no snake,' exclaimed Mum. 'That's Chitty's exhaust. We're getting warmer.'

'On the one hand,' said Dad, 'that's good news. On the other, it does mean that bits are falling off Chitty. Keep an eye open, everyone. We can't afford to lose any of her parts.'

The next few hundred yards of squeezing and scrambling took hours. On the way they gathered up one of Chitty's door handles, a spring from her upholstery, her toolbox and her back bumper. All the time, the roaring got louder and louder. They came to a place where the ground rose almost vertically for twenty feet. The motorway noise was deafening now.

'We could climb up the tree and get on to the top of the bank this way,' said Mum, shinning up the nearest trunk. 'It's not as hard as it looks,' she called. 'All you have to do is . . . Oh.'

'Mum?'

'*Mum?*'

There was no answer. Dad went straight up the tree trunk after her, lugging bits of Chitty with him.

'Can you see her? Is she all right?' called Jem.

'She's . . . Oh,' called Dad.

Then there was silence again.

Little Harry and Jem and then Lucy and Red swarmed up the trunk to see what had happened. But when they got to the top, they too could only think of one thing to say. Namely, 'Oh.'

The noise that they had heard rumbling down the hillside and through the jungle was not a motorway. It was a waterfall. The highest waterfall anyone on this planet has ever seen. So high that its top was lost in the clouds. Looking up at it, it seemed that heaven had sprung a leak. Water fell like a vertical river, fell so far that most of it spread into a curtain of mist on the way down. Then dropped into a wide, black chasm in the side of the mountain. Bridging that chasm, shrouded in mist from the thundering water, was something more amazing even than that amazing cascade. It was a town. A town of houses and streets and towers and gardens. A town that arched like a rainbow across the deep black cliffs. A town that shone like a sunset.

A town whose buildings were made entirely of gold.

137

10

'El Dorado – the city of gold,' gasped Jem. 'I thought it was just a story.'

'The Queen thought Chitty was just a story,' said Lucy. 'But we turned out to be real. Now the lost city of Eldorado turns out to be not so lost after all.'

'Your father is so clever,' smiled Mum. 'Some people can't even find their own lost car keys. Your father has found a legendary lost city of gold.'

'Obviously it's quite exciting that we've found a legendary lost city of gold,' said Jem. 'But we must remember it's not what we were looking for.'

'Isn't that always the way,' said Mum. 'You're looking for one thing but you find something else altogether. It's the same when you lose your car keys and find your phone as it is when you lose a time-travelling car and find a legendary city of gold.'

'This place must be worth a lot more than twenty-five dollars,' said Red. 'It's got to be worth a hundred dollars at least.'

'A hundred million dollars would be nearer the mark,' said Lucy.

'But what we really need is Chitty,' said Jem.

A haze of tiny droplets from the waterfall wrapped the town in a mist, like tissue paper. Even though the street seemed to be deserted, it was full of movement. There were ghostly presences everywhere – shadows dancing on the mist, reflections washing across the golden walls, hummingbirds flirting and whirring, and the waterfall roaring like an invisible football crowd. The first building they came to was a little domed house with a sign on the door that read:

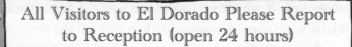

All Visitors to El Dorado Please Report to Reception (open 24 hours)

Dad pushed open the golden door, which was warm to touch and which moved on its hinges as smoothly and silently as silk. He stepped inside. They crowded in after him and the door swished shut. The dome was made of gold that was beaten as thin as paper. Sunlight poured through it, making everything it touched glow golden. Mum and Dad looked like statues. The long, thick, curling things on the floor looked like golden pillows and cushions. Except that they were moving. Not to mention hissing.

'Oh, for heaven's sake,' huffed Mum, 'not MORE snakes!'

There were half a dozen hungry anacondas in there.

Dad put down the parts of Chitty he was carrying and tried the door, but there was no handle on the inside.

'Reception' wasn't reception at all. It was a trap.

'This must definitely be the unspeakable fate of the Pott family,' said Lucy. 'Digested in a walk-in snake-pit. If we look around we'll find their bones. Then we'll die.' As she said this, one of the snakes tried to gulp down her arm.

'This is so annoying,' said Mum, rolling up her sleeves. 'Come on, everyone, lend a hand.'

The Tooting family spent the next ten minutes anaconda-wrestling. Every now and then Mum would coach them – shouting tips or showing them new grips. 'Watch your dad,' she'd say. 'He's unbeatable.'

It was Red who spotted the last undefeated snake trying to sneak off down a little tunnel. When he dragged it back into the pit by its tail, he found that it had a piece of rope clamped between its jaws. When Red pulled it, bells rang merrily somewhere overhead.

'It must be some sort of alarm,' said Jem.

Within a few seconds, the door opened and in walked the Queen.

'How absolutely lovely of you to call,' said Imogen, scooping up the last conscious snake and draping it round her neck.

'Welcome to El Dorado,' said Eliza. 'I see you have already met our pets.'

'They tried to eat us,' said Mum.

'You mustn't be cross with them. They're trained to eat visitors,' said Eliza.

'Absolutely trained to. Trained them ourselves,' said Imogen.

'We have to keep El Dorado a secret,' explained Eliza, 'and snakes seemed much the best way to do it.'

'That doesn't work with us,' said Mum. 'No snake alive could defeat my husband.'

'Please,' said Dad, who was still trying to get his breath back. 'You took our car. We need it back.'

Imogen and Eliza looked shocked. 'You can't ask

for a present back once you've given it. That's the height of rudeness, isn't it, Imogen?' said Eliza.

'Height *and* depth of it,' said Imogen. 'Don't be so rude.'

'I think you'll find,' said Mum, 'that the height of rudeness is trying to feed your guests to snakes.'

'Anyway,' said Dad, 'we didn't give you the car as a present. You just took it.'

'Well now, there's a reason for that, isn't there, Imogen?'

'There certainly is. When you came to us, we gave you all kinds of presents. Whatever you said you liked, we gave you.'

'Which is only polite.'

'If someone admires something, it's only polite to give it to them.'

'And we admired Chitty Chitty Bang Bang like billy-o.'

'We admired her twice.'

'But you never gave her to us.'

'Not so much as her spare tyre.'

'That was rude.'

'That was unusually rude.'

'But our great-grandmother always said, "When someone is rude, just ignore them."'

'So we ignored your rudeness.'

'And we took Chitty. Simple.'

'It was simple till you tried to feed us to anacondas.'

'We are a bit unpredictable at times.'

'Would you like a tour of El Dorado? We're ever so proud of it.'

'Ever so, ever so.'

Everyone followed the unpredictable Queen out of the snake-pit and into the streets of gold. Whenever they passed a house, windows would open and people would lean out and wave to the Queen. Or they would come running out of their front doors to tell them news. Or share problems. A couple of times the Queen had to stop to examine a door that wouldn't shut properly or a dripping tap. Dad had brought Chitty's toolbox so he was happy to help.

In the middle of the town square, mounted on a pedestal of gold, was a diamond as big as your head.

'What's that?' asked Red.

'That,' said Imogen, 'is a diamond as big as your head.'

'We call it,' said Eliza, 'the Diamond As Big As Your Head. In the evening we come down here and watch the changing reflections of the sunset play in the depths of the diamond's heart.'

'It's like a very early form of television,' said

Lucy. 'A very early, unbelievably expensive and slightly abstract form of television.'

'What's television?' asked Red.

The square led to a platform that jutted right out over the waterfall. From here they could see the whole rainforest and the great Orinoco River winding through it, as clearly as if it had been drawn on a map.

'This is where we were standing,' said Imogen, 'when we first saw Chitty heading upriver towards us.'

'I had to dash off,' said Eliza, 'and get everyone to go back down to the village made of wood so we could pretend that we all lived there.'

'Why?'

'People are always looking for El Dorado, City of Gold. If they find a perfectly nice city of wood where the City of Gold is supposed to be, it puts them off the scent.'

'But it is so much stress.'

'Such stress,' agreed Imogen. 'That's why you have to be two people to be Queen. Because El Dorado is two towns. One real and one pretend.'

'But why?' asked Lucy. 'A town made of gold should be one of the wonders of the world.'

'If I had all this gold,' said Red, 'I wouldn't want anyone to see it. I'd keep it all to myself too. Hats off to you, girls, you're doing the right thing.'

'It's simple really,' said Imogen. 'El Dorado – City of Gold – used to be spread out all along the riverbank. But, as you know, people here love to give presents and get presents. People gave us all kinds of things – fish, pots, pigs, boats . . .'

'Those leaves that make your head feel funny when you chew them.'

'They were fun. But all people wanted in return was gold. Everyone wanted gold.'

ALL THE GOLD IN THE WORLD! (SO FAR DISCOVERED)

'We didn't mind giving them a bit of gold, of course, Eliza.'

'No, of course not, but gold is so useful, you know, for plumbing and roofing. It's easy to cut. It's not too cold and best of all it doesn't go rusty.'

'We'd just got the town how we liked it . . .'

'. . . when people started taking it away, bit by bit. Imagine.'

'Imagine people coming round taking your roof. Or your downspout.'

'But we hated to offend anyone by saying, "No, you can't have our golden downspout."'

'Or our golden roof.'

'So we moved the whole golden town up to the waterfall and pretended that all our gold had gone.'

'It's nice that no one is offended.'

'But it's such stress pretending to live in one

147

place when you really live somewhere else.'

'Double stress,' agreed Eliza.

'Double stress multiplied by both of us,' said Imogen.

'But now we've got Chitty. She will sort out all our problems.'

'That's what our great-grandmother promised us. "Chitty Chitty will come back," she said, "and solve all your problems."'

'And she never lied.'

'Well, well, pip-pip, must go and rule,' said Imogen.

'Pip-pip, rule-rule,' said Eliza. 'A monarch's work is never done.'

From the golden platform, the Tootings looked out over the unending jungle.

'What are we going to do?' said Jem.

'Search the city until we find Chitty,' said Dad. 'Then go straight back home, where no one tries to feed you to the snakes.'

'We're in a legendary city of gold,' said Mum. 'The least we can do is take some photographs. Lucy . . .'

Lucy took out her jelly phone, then almost dropped it. Staring at her from the screen was Nanny.

'Well, well, well,' smiled Nanny. 'Look where you are! The legendary Lost City of Gold. You know what I think? I think the moment Tiny Jack gets his hand on Chitty, that will be the first place he'll go. He just loves gold, bless his heart. He'll go straight there and he'll bring every scrap home.'

'Home?' said Dad.

'That's what we call Zborowski Terrace now. We just love it here. It's so cosy!'

Lucy hung up.

'Don't answer it any more,' said Mum. 'It upsets your father.'

'I didn't answer it then,' said Lucy. 'Somehow she was there waiting for me when I picked it up.'

'That was a good idea about taking the gold away,' said Red. 'We could take a truckload and whoop it up in Manhattan. Then when it's all gone, come back, get another truckload and whoop it up again.'

'Somehow I don't think the Queen is going to let us get away with that,' said Lucy. 'We have to do things their way.'

'What do you mean?'

'We have to give them presents. If we give them good enough presents, they just might give Chitty back.'

'But we don't have any presents,' said Mum.

'We're from the future,' said Jem. 'We must have something that they would think was amazing. What about Little Harry's remote-control dinosaur? I bet they'd think that was worth a Chitty.'

'Brilliant idea!' said Dad.

Little Harry knew straight away what they were talking about. He clutched his little red backpack to his chest and said, 'No, no, no.'

'We'll find you another one,' soothed Mum, 'as soon as we get home. Two in fact . . .' But when she got the backpack open, there was no dinosaur in there. 'What happened? Did you leave it in Chitty? Did you lose it in New York?'

Little Harry was crying. Mum cuddled him while the others tried to think of presents.

'What about this sticky spider's web stuff?' said Jem. 'It's so strong and thin at the same time.'

'The rainforest is full of spiders,' said Lucy. 'They could pick as much of that stuff as they liked off the trees.'

'It breaks my heart to say this,' said Red, reaching into his pocket, 'but do you think they'd sell it to us? I've got nearly ten dollars . . .'

'Oh, Red,' said Mum, 'that's the sweetest thing I ever heard.' She kissed his cheek. He blushed. 'But it won't work. They don't use money. They think it's silly.'

'Yeah, but they're wrong. Money is the greatest. If we explained it to them . . .'

'No,' said Dad, 'that won't work. What we need is a shop or an all-night garage. Somewhere we could buy a big box of chocolates.'

'We're in sixteenth-century Amazonia, Dad. There are no all-night garages,' said Lucy, 'but you've given me an idea. Jem, where's the logbook?'

Lucy flicked quickly through the pages of the logbook, which Jem had handed to her, until she came to 'Monsieur Bon Bon's Secret Fooj Formula'.

'I thought that was some kind of racing fuel,' said Jem, 'but Mum said it was . . .'

'Fudge,' said Lucy. 'It's a recipe for fudge. Follow me.'

They followed her to the nearest house. A family was sitting around outside, playing a game with little glass balls.

'Are they diamonds?' gasped Red. 'Can I see?'

Lucy said something to them in a language the others didn't understand.

'I thought you said that you didn't speak El Doradoan,' said Dad.

'That was this morning,' said Lucy. 'I've had all day to learn.'

'What did you tell them?'

'I told them I liked their stove. Also their pots

151

and pans. They said we could have them.'

'What do you want their stove for? You can't leave a family with no cooker.'

'They can have it back in an hour.'

The stove was in a courtyard, overhung with branches and blossom, around the back of the house. Lucy gathered the ingredients and pans she needed. The secret of Monsieur Bon Bon's secret fudge recipe is

TOP SECRET

This makes the fudge come out smooth and creamy instead of gritty and sugary. Lucy set to work.

'Lucy?' gasped Mum. 'Are you cooking?' Lucy had never cooked anything before in her life.

'Think of it as an experiment in economics,' said Lucy, 'which just happens to be edible.'

'It won't be edible if you let the pan bubble like that. It will be burned.'

'I'm following instructions.'

'The instructions involve a certain amount of familiarity with the concept of not incinerating things.'

The thick, black, tarry mixture in the bottom of the pan did look fairly unconvincing. Lucy started again. This time she read out the instructions and measured the quantities while Mum stirred and mixed and blended. Soon the pan was bubbling again and soon after that faces began to appear, peeping over the courtyard wall. All over El Dorado people dropped what they were doing and drifted towards the smell. It was as if their brains had allowed their noses to take control of their bodies.

Dad opened the gate so that people could come in and see the fudge. For a while, they stood there, smelling it in silence, while Mum poured it on to a tray to cool. They had no idea it was something you could eat. It smelt so good that just smelling it was enough. No one even thought of eating it. As that lovely fudge fragrance floated out across the city in tattered wisps of steam, out across the treetops, all the squirrels, bats and monkeys stopped what they were doing and sniffed the air. The whole forest fell silent.

When Lucy finally picked up a piece and popped it into her mouth, everyone lunged forward. She put up her hand and said, 'Surely your Queen eats first.'

'Surely the Queen eats last,' said Imogen.

'Normally yes,' said Eliza, 'but on this occasion . . .'

Hungrily, she reached for the fudge. Mum pulled it out of her way. 'I think it probably needs to set,' she said, 'to bring out its true creaminess.'

The waterfall itself seemed to wait with bated breath until the fudge had set to perfection. Then Mum said, 'OK, it's ready,' and with a great shout, the Great Amazonian Fudge stampede began. Elbows, knees, shins and fists flew as everyone tussled to grab a piece. The city reverberated to the sound of happy chewing and contented sucking. This is when Lucy announced her great idea.

'Your Majesty,' she said, 'and people of El Dorado. What you are eating not only tastes delicious, it is also the answer to all the problems of El Dorado. El Dorado is made of gold but people from out of town like that gold and want to take it away. Because you are polite and lovely you feel you have to give away your own doors and gutters and roofs as presents.'

'Stress,' sighed Eliza.

'Solid-gold stress,' agreed Imogen.

'What El Dorado needs – what this whole beautiful forest needs – is something that its people will like more than gold. Ladies and gentlemen, Your Majesty, I give you . . . fudge.'

'Oh!' said everyone. 'Definitely.'

'But,' said Imogen, 'what happens when we run out of fudge? There're already only –' she counted – '. . . thirty-seven slices left. And I want one.'

'The magic of fudge,' said Lucy, 'is that you don't dig it out of the ground. You make it. You can make as much of it as you like. This is Monsieur Bon Bon's Secret Fooj Formula. With this recipe, you will have an infinite, inexhaustible supply of fudge . . .'

'Wait,' said Eliza. 'You mean we can eat this more than once in our lives?'

'You can eat this every day. You can share it

with everyone who comes to visit.'

'No one will ever want our gold again,' said Eliza.

'Who would want gold when they could eat fudge?' said Imogen.

'Chitty Chitty Bang Bang, or at least her logbook,' said Lucy, 'has solved all your problems. She has moved you from a gold-based economy to a fudge-based economy. Which is loads better. In a fudge-based economy no one ever has to be poor. In a gold-based economy you can run out of gold. In the fudge-based economy, if you run out of fudge – make some more fudge. Your stress is at an end.'

'You've solved all our social and economic problems,' said Eliza.

'We must give her a present,' whispered Imogen.

'We've got just the thing,' said Eliza.

'Follow the monarch,' said Imogen, leading the way down a wide avenue of trees. A troupe of little monkeys clattered through the branches above their heads.

'In there,' said Imogen, pointing to what seemed to be a small, golden garage.

'Look inside, look inside,' said Eliza.

Dad was the first to open the door, the first to see – spread out on the earthy floor – a pile of springs and wires and valves and lightbulbs, gaskets and bolts and nuts.

'What is it?' asked Mum.

'I know what it is,' said Jem, who recognized every single nut, bolt and clip.

'Me too,' said Dad.

'That,' said Jem, 'is Chitty Chitty Bang Bang.'

'Well, this solves the mystery of how they got her through the jungle,' said Lucy. 'They took her completely to pieces, then left the pieces in a heap.'

If you've ever come home to find that someone has taken your house apart piece by piece, leaving nothing but a neat pile of bricks and a stack of floorboards, you'll have some idea of how the Tootings felt looking at that heap of spare parts. For a long time, they didn't speak or move, but stood in silence, each thinking their private thoughts. Mum remembered the day they found the headlights on top of the Eiffel Tower. Now those headlights were lying on their side on the earth floor. Jem remembered the day he first saw Chitty's wings, carving through the sky above the cliffs of Dover. Now those wings lay against the carburettor like a pair of old deckchairs. Dad remembered where he had first seen that big, beautiful beast of an engine – stuck in a tree in a scrapyard. Now here was Chitty in a thousand pieces as though she had just fallen down from that tree, as though all the adventures they had had together were nothing but a dream.

'I must say,' said Imogen, 'I thought you'd be more pleased.'

'We brought her all this way,' said Eliza.

'But you took her to pieces,' said Red. 'How are we going to win the race now? It'll take years to put her back together again.'

'Oh, we don't mind that,' said Imogen.

'We waited years for her to come back.'

'Years and years.'

'We're happy for you to spend years fixing her.'

'Well, well, must go and rule,' said Imogen.

'A ruler's work is never done,' sighed Eliza, and off they went.

Dad and Jem surveyed Chitty's scattered components. 'Here's the starter motor,' whooped Dad, scooping it up from under Mum's feet.

'Don't bother,' growled Red. 'That car's not broken, it's destroyed.'

'Dad will put her back together in no time,' said Jem.

'What? With those fat fingers? I doubt it.'

'Those fat fingers,' snapped Mum, 'rebuilt Chitty Chitty Bang Bang from scratch with no help from anyone.'

'Actually I got a lot of help from Jem,' admitted Dad. 'Not to mention Professor Tuk-Tuk . . .'

'My husband took a rusty old engine stuck up a tree and he turned it into the most beautiful car this world has ever seen.'

'Stuck up a tree?' said Red.

'Stuck up a tree,' repeated Mum, 'in Basildon. That was just the engine. The headlights were in Paris. The bodywork was on the shores of the Indian Ocean. The wheels were in the Sahara Desert . . .'

'Why?' asked Red. 'How did that happen?'

'That's a mystery I'm always trying to solve,' said Jem. 'You see, when you think about it . . .'

'I knew it!' said Dad, who'd been examining the starter motor all this time. 'The carbon brushes and the end plates don't contact properly. If we can sort this out, we won't need to get champagne whenever she doesn't start. And there's the rear end seal. I've always had my doubts about that. We should strip out the transmission while we are here. You know, this could be the ideal opportunity for us to make Chitty better than ever.'

'Ga gooo ga!' went Chitty's klaxon, suddenly making everyone jump.

'Chitty agrees!' said Mum.

'What Chitty? There is no Chitty,' growled Red. 'There's a pile of parts.'

'If there's one thing we've learned,' said Jem, 'it's that Chitty is a lot more than the sum of her parts.'

Dad offered to let Red help him and Jem rebuild the most beautiful and technologically advanced vehicle ever made.

'How much will you give me?' said Red.

'Nothing,' said Dad.

'Then no,' said Red.

So Dad and Jem spent days classifying nuts and bolts and cogs and screws. Days that reminded them of last summer – or of a summer five hundred years in the future, depending on how you look at it – when they had first rebuilt a camper van together. Back then they had sometimes spent a whole morning discussing where one piece of tubing should go, sometimes a day in silence, slotting this part into the other. Back then, Mum had brought them snacks and drinks whenever they looked tired. She did the same now. The snacks were slightly different though: instead of cakes and tea, they were mostly baked snakes or pan-fried tarantulas that she'd caught while out trekking in the jungle with Imogen and Eliza.

'Food was so dull before Chitty came back,' said Imogen.

'So very dull,' agreed Eliza.

'Now we have baked snake in fudge sauce.'

'And pan-fried tarantula in fudge sauce.'

'And sometimes fudge in fudge sauce.'

'And sometimes just fudge.'

During the long misty days while Dad and Jem were rebuilding Chitty, Mum and Lucy (and Little Harry) questioned all the old people in town, to see if they had any memory of where the Potts might have gone. They all said the same thing: 'They went. They said they'd be back soon. But they never came back.'

They searched the forest for some sign or clue. The Queen came with them to make sure they didn't disappear like the Potts. But it was hopeless. The forest was so vast. And also so full of distractions.

Every time they saw an anaconda, Mum felt she had to wrestle it.

'I'm sorry, but I just had no idea I had such a natural talent for anaconda-wrestling.'

'Don't apologize,' said Eliza. 'Nothing we like to watch more than a bit of anaconda-wrestling. Is there, Imogen?'

'Unless it's jaguar-punching,' said Imogen. 'We love jaguar-punching too.'

'I must say now that we know how good you are at wrestling them, we don't feel so bad that we tried to kill you with anacondas.'

'That does make it more forgivable,' said Mum.

'Then we are friends?'

'I suppose we are.'

Those days spent high in the cloud forest were the most magical of all their adventures. Every morning they woke to the sound of the happiest, noisiest dawn chorus that they had ever heard. The sun lavished its warmth and light upon them, but thanks to the spray from the waterfall it was never too hot. In the evening, they would join the people in the square and watch the colours of sunset dancing in the facets of the Diamond As Big As Your Head.

Red meanwhile taught all the children of El Dorado to play hide-and-seek.

'I'm not sure,' said Lucy, 'a trackless equatorial wilderness on the brink of an unbelievably high waterfall is the best place for a game of hide-and-seek. People could get hurt. Or horribly maimed. Or go missing for years on end. Or be eaten by jaguars. Or piranhas. Or plunge to their doom.'

'That's what makes it so good,' said Red. 'It kind of gives it an edge.'

'As soon as Chitty is back to her old self,' said Dad one evening when – yet again – Mum and Lucy had returned with no sign of the Potts, 'we'll fly all over the forest until we find them. Then we'll go and deal with Tiny Jack and Nanny.'

Next day, while Dad and Jem worked, Little Harry sat up on the seat in front of the steering wheel and pulled it this way and that. 'Chitty Chitty Bang Bang!' he yelled.

He's right, thought Jem. She is beginning to look like that unique Paragon Panther.

'Ga gooo ga!' honked Chitty.

'There are a few bits and pieces I don't recognize,' said Dad. 'This glass dome, for instance. And this metal cone. Also there seem to be two extra engines. Or maybe they're not engines. They look more like atomic hairdryers. I never noticed them before. They must have been lodged under the back wheel arches or maybe they're from the village and they just got . . .'

'If only we could ask Chitty where they go,' said Jem. 'Sometimes, when you drive her, don't you feel she's trying to tell you something? When you talk to her, do you sometimes feel that she's going to answer back?'

'No,' said Dad. 'Let's just stick these things in wherever they fit and hope for the best. You know, I could live like this – just sitting around repairing classic motor cars in sixteenth-century El Dorado.'

As the sun went down over the rainforest that evening, Dad and Jem fitted the last rivet. Jem cranked the engine and Dad pressed the starter motor. She started first time.

'Tomorrow,' he said, 'we'll begin our aerial search for the Pott family. Now let's get some food.'

Dad went to cook supper, but Jem sat for a while, leaning against Chitty's wheel arch as the bats skittered through the twilight. 'Goodnight, Chitty,' he whispered. The car did not speak but Jem could hear the metal of her pipes cooling in the chill night air, the oil and the water settling down, and he knew that she was restless to go. As he walked through the moonlit golden streets, he thought he heard the softest goodbye snuffle from her klaxon. But it could have been a pangolin looking for ants.

Next morning, when Jem woke up, Chitty had vanished.

'Not again!' groaned Mum.

'Don't worry,' said Imogen, 'it was us.'

'It was you last time,' said Mum.

'We thought she didn't quite fit in with the town . . .'

'All that green and silver, it clashed with the brickwork.'

'So we sent her away . . .'

'Where to?'

'Oh. Not *away* away, just . . .'

From somewhere behind them they heard 'Ga gooo ga!'

There was Chitty, a crowd of happy El Doradoan children pushing her towards them.

'What have you done to her?' gasped Dad.

'Can't you tell?' said Imogen.

'Isn't it obvious?' said Eliza.

Chitty did look different. Very different. Smarter. Shinier.

'We've had her covered with gold,' said Imogen.

'*You gilded Chitty?*'

'What do you think?' asked Eliza.

'Do you like it?' said Imogen.

'It's very shiny,' said Mum. 'Sort of, Chitty Chitty Bling Bling.'

'At least like this you will be taking a little piece of El Dorado with you, wherever you go. Goodbye. It's very hard to say goodbye to such good friends.'

'Oh, we're not leaving yet,' said Dad. 'We're going to search the river and the jungle for signs of the Pott family.'

'We have to find them,' said Mum. 'We need their help. The whole planet could be in incredible danger.'

'What's wrong with incredible danger?' said Imogen.

'We love incredible danger, don't we, Imogen?' said Eliza.

'Chitty always has somewhere to go,' sighed Imogen.

'One day she will leave you too.'

'I think,' gasped Jem, 'she's trying to leave us right now. Run!' Somehow Chitty had slipped her handbrake and was rolling towards the edge of the cliff. The Tootings ran after her and jumped on board.

'Wait! Where's Red?' yelled Jem.

Just in time, Red came tearing out of the forest, flung himself into the back of the car and yelled, 'Den! I won!' He looked back at the woods to see if anyone was behind him. He was so happy to have won his one hundred and seventh consecutive game of Extreme Hide-and-Seek (with jaguars) that he barely noticed that Chitty had leaped from the ledge and was soaring above the waterfall. He barely heard the cheers and whoops of the El Doradoans as they waved and shouted their goodbyes and their thank-yous.

Chitty curved through the air above the abyss, and came round in a wide, lazy circle, bringing them face to face with the full force of the waterfall

as it fell. Everyone caught their breath – partly because it was so amazing, partly because the spray from the fall was so fresh and so cold.

'It looks like a lovely gold brooch,' cried Red. 'Where are we going?'

Hot air from the rainforest rises in great columns, called thermals. Birds such as condors and vultures use these to lift them higher and higher into the air. Today – do as Dad might – Chitty rolled from thermal to thermal, like a huge mechanical condor, rising and rising in great circles as though she was climbing an invisible spiral staircase.

'Look,' yelled Jem, as they finally rolled over the very top of the great waterfall. Below them was a vast, almost perfectly circular lake. There was nothing higher than it for miles around. It was like an eye looking straight into the sky.

'Where's El Dorado gone?' asked Red.

'Over that way somewhere. Under the clouds.'

'You mean we're higher than the clouds?'

'Yes. A lot higher . . . Look.'

A flock of puffy white clouds passed far beneath them. Through a gap they glimpsed a tiny flicker of light, like the flash of a camera. It was all that could be seen of El Dorado.

'I bet we're the first people ever to see that lake,' said Lucy. 'I bet no one will see it again for hundreds of years.'

'We are way too high,' said Red. 'Take us down! Take us down!' He reached over the front seat for one of the handles.

'Red! Don't touch anything. You don't know which switch does what!'

Too late. He had already grabbed the Chronojuster. El Dorado disappeared in a flicker of nights and days and weeks and months.

No one who wasn't born in El Dorado ever saw the City of Gold again.

11

History rippled past the Tooting family like the pages in a flicker book, until they found themselves gliding gently down into what seemed to be a waving green ocean.

'Grass?' gasped Dad. 'It's grass. How can there be this much grass? Red, what have you done? This isn't Basildon.'

'It wasn't Red's fault,' said Jem.

'What? He pulled the Chronojuster.'

Dad had brought Chitty down gently on a dusty road that ran across a prairie. Small brown islands looked up as he landed. These turned out to be grazing buffalo. They watched Chitty, then carried on chewing as Dad drove her forward.

'The Chronojuster was glowing,' said Jem. 'Naturally, Red grabbed it. But who made it glow?

Chitty did. Chitty brought us here. Why?'

The moment he asked the question, a massive old car thundered past them, whipping up clouds of dust and belching smoke from its gleaming exhausts. Jem looked behind just in time to see another car racing up behind them.

'That's the answer to your question,' said Lucy. 'The juxtaposition of fast cars and buffalo suggests to me that we are on the Kansas leg of the Prix d'Esmerelda Birthday Cake. Fasten your seat belts, everyone!'

Chitty leaped forward and was soon alongside the car in front – a huge, royal-blue gondola with wheels that seemed to crush the stones beneath them. The driver scowled from behind a fabulously curly moustache as he pressed harder on the accelerator, trying to keep up with Chitty. But Chitty soon slipped past him and did what she often did when she overtook another car: cheekily waggled her back fender and gave him a triumphant blast of her deafening klaxon.

'Honestly, she's so undignified,' sighed Lucy.

The Kansas sunlight blazed off Chitty's golden bodywork, so that they felt they were travelling inside a comet

'What's that?' yelled Jem.

Far, far ahead they could just make out a tiny

white dot in the middle of the road. No matter how fast Chitty went, the white dot did not seem to get any bigger. It was moving as fast as they were. It could only be one thing: Chitty the Second.

'The Count!' said Lucy. 'Are we going to catch up with him?'

'Probably not,' said Dad. 'The brand-new Chitty seems to be faster than the dear old Chitty.' As if in answer to this slight, Chitty's engine revved furiously and a switch on her dashboard glowed like an angry fairy light. 'I've never noticed that switch before,' said Dad. 'I wonder what it is?'

'Chitty is trying to tell us something,' said Jem.

'Shall I flick the switch?'

'What if it's that ejector-seat thing again?' said Red.

But before anyone had time to consider this possibility, Dad flicked the switch. Everything happened so fast that at first everyone thought it really *was* the ejector seat.

The horizon rushed towards them. They felt they were falling. Kansas was a blur of green. Sheer speed shoved all of them back into their seats. The tiny white dot became a white marble, then a white tennis ball, then a white football.

'I think we've just discovered what those funny

little extra engine things were for,' said Dad, through gritted teeth.

Seconds later, the white football-sized object had become a gleaming white racing car. They were slipping past the elegant, aerodynamic form of Chitty the Second. Chitty herself (the Original and Best Chitty) slowed right down, as though to allow her rival to get a good look at her new gleaming gold bodywork.

'I say!' yelled the Count. But before he could say anything specific, Chitty thundered past, waggled her fender and sounded her victory klaxon.

'So embarrassing,' sighed Lucy.

On they raced towards the finishing line, leaving Chitty the Second far, far behind.

Fifty-six minutes and thirty-seven seconds later, Red was basking in the sunlight reflected in Chitty's bodywork. 'Look at my arm,' he said. 'It's like I'm made of gold.'

Then all at once, the sun was snuffed out. Jem looked up and saw the undercarriage of a plane, just a few feet above their heads, keeping perfect pace with Chitty, who had slowed down now that she had an insurmountable lead. As they watched, a ladder was lowered and down it came the elegant figure of Count Zborowski's butler, Crackitt. He hung from the ladder, just alongside Chitty, and, with a smooth nod of the head, passed Mum a letter before climbing back up to the cockpit.

Mum opened the letter.

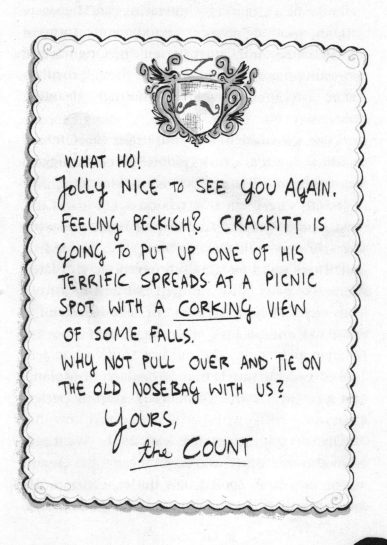

WHAT HO!
Jolly NICE TO SEE YOU AGAIN.
FEELING PECKISH? CRACKITT IS
GOING TO PUT UP ONE OF HIS
TERRIFIC SPREADS AT A PICNIC
SPOT WITH A <u>CORKING</u> VIEW
OF SOME FALLS.
WHY NOT PULL OVER AND TIE ON
THE OLD NOSEBAG WITH US?
    Yours,
        the COUNT

'Stop for a picnic? Are you nuts?' cried Red. 'We can win this race.'

'Actually I am quite hungry,' admitted Dad.

'And a picnic could be really nice,' said Lucy.

'Lucy, you hate picnics,' said Mum. 'You always say sunshine and laughter are the two most depressing things in the world.'

But just after they drove through the next town, they saw Crackitt's lovely yellow biplane parked in the shade of a copse of trees. Crackitt was standing to attention, a crisp white cloth draped over his arm and, at his feet, a wide gingham tablecloth spread out over the grass. On it was the most fabulous picnic that any of them had ever seen. No one could have driven past a picnic like that. There was a pie almost a foot deep. Its pastry shone like glass. Steam drifted lazily from a hole in its crust. There were piles of crusty bread, huge chunks of cheese, jugs of lemonade and a bucket full of grapes.

'His Lordship insists that you start without him,' said Crackitt, as the Tootings clambered out of Chitty.

'Oh, we couldn't do that,' said Mum. 'We'll just enjoy the view until he comes.'

The others all agreed. But the view that most interested them was not the one of the waterfall but the one of that beautiful pie. It was a view that filled them with anxiety. What if someone stole it? What if there was an earthquake and the earth itself swallowed it?

'His Lordship really was most insistent that you start,' said Crackitt.

'Oh, if he insists,' said Dad. He dived on that pie, sliced it up and passed it round so quickly that lightning itself would not have got a look in.

'Save some for the Count!' said Lucy.

But she needn't have worried. Each slice was so densely packed with meat, so bursting with flavour, that a mouthful was enough to keep their tastebuds busy for hours. They savoured their slices while the sun slid over the horizon. Dusk was turning into night when Chitty the Second finally rolled up.

'I say,' said the Count. 'This is something! What a lovely spot. Pop a couple of tents up, Crackitt, and we'll pass the night here.'

A yellow moon was

high in the sky by the time they finished the picnic. The Count gave them all the news about the Prix d'Esmerelda.

'It's gone marvellously well. We're on for a record-breaking time.'

'What's the current record?' asked Lucy.

'Six months.'

'Six *months*?'

'Yes, but it looks like I'm going to do it in five months, three weeks and four days.'

'But these cars go so fast. How has it taken so long?'

'They do go very fast,' said the Count. 'But they will keep on running out of petrol. Then you have to find petrol and sometimes there are no garages nearby. Sometimes there are no *people* nearby. In Texas we ended up having to dig for oil. Luckily I found quite a good oilfield, so that's a few more bob in the bank. There were one or two other delays on the way. Kidnapped by bandits in New Mexico, for instance.'

'Bandits!' whooped Little Harry, causing Jem to look around nervously.

'Were you in terrible danger?' gasped Lucy.

'Oh, they were frightfully nice chaps once I'd paid the old ransom. Then there was the whole business with the Grand Canyon.'

'The Grand Canyon? What happened there?' asked Lucy.

'Well, the Grand Canyon is surprisingly large. And also quite a few feet deep. As holes in the road go, it must be one of the biggest. They say you can't miss it. But what if you *want* to miss it? A sign saying

If You Go Any Further You'll Fall In

might have been useful. Then there were tornadoes too. Bears in Colorado. It's been quite a packed five months, three weeks and four days. But now we're almost home. Tomorrow we should cross the finishing line. And it looks like we're the two front runners. How on earth did you get ahead of me? I haven't seen you since the Catskill Mountains.'

'We took a detour,' said Dad.

'May the best man win tomorrow. Or the best girl of course. 'Night, all. Must get the old head down.' He got up to stroll back to his tent, but before taking a step, he said, 'I say! What's that?'

'That,' said Lucy, 'is the moon.'

'Do you know, they've got a moon exactly like that one down in New Mexico.'

'That's actually the same moon,' said Lucy. 'You

can see it here the same as you can in New Mexico.'

'Are you absolutely sure about that? New Mexico is a dashed long way from here.'

Lucy tried to explain lunar orbits to the Count, using a tangerine and an Edam cheese she picked up from the picnic.

The Count looked deep into her eyes and said, 'Lucy, of all the girls I've met on all my travels, you are certainly the most . . . what's the word?'

Lucy tried to imagine what the word might be – 'beautiful'? 'mysterious'? 'poetic'? 'brilliant'?

'Informative,' said the Count. 'You're by far the most informative girl I've ever met. I say, do you fancy taking a spin with me tomorrow in Chitty the Second? With you in the passenger seat, we'd be sure to win the race.'

'Yes, please,' said Lucy, straight away.

'I thought,' said the Count, 'that you might need time to think about it.'

'I'm a very quick thinker.'

Next morning Lucy woke up to the sound of engines. Some of the other cars in the race had finally caught up with them and were thundering past the picnic site.

'We'd better wake the Count,' she said.

'Lucy, wait . . .' It was Jem. He was crouched next

to her sleeping bag, with Chitty's logbook open on his knee and a haggard, worried look on his face. He hadn't slept all night. 'There's something I want to show you.'

'We'll be late for the race.'

'It's important. Don't wake the others. Not yet. I was going through the logbook, trying to figure out why Chitty had brought us here.'

'It's obvious, isn't it? She wants to teach Chitty the Second a lesson. That's why we went to El Dorado so she could have her golden makeover and then come back and win the race.'

'That's what I thought. I was thinking how terrible it would be if we'd been through all these dangers just so that she could win a race. I was wondering if there was any way we could understand what she was thinking or make her understand what *we* are thinking, when I found this . . .'

A page from the *Encyclopaedia Britannica* had been glued into the logbook and folded over. Jem opened it. It was a page about Count Louis Zborowski.

'Commander Pott must have put it there. I think he was trying to find out as much about the history of Chitty as he possibly good.'

'It's Louis! That's a terrible photograph of him. Ha! His middle name was Elliot. Who knew?' She tried to take the book from him but Jem nudged it away from her. 'What else does it tell you?'

'It says here,' he said, 'that he died.'

Lucy swallowed hard. Then she shrugged. 'Well, of course he died. Everyone dies. If he'd lived until our time he'd be . . .'

'A hundred and twenty,' said Jem.

'Exactly. Who lives to be a hundred and twenty? Who'd want to live to a hundred and twenty? You know one thing I like to do while we're time travelling is look at all the people we meet and think about the fact they're all dead. That they're sort of ghosts. It's really melancholy, which is great. I look at the Count and think: You probably died in the war doing something heroic, or maybe you were killed in a duel or something.'

'Or a race.'

'Exactly. A high-speed collision as he broke a world speed record.'

'A race like this one.'

Lucy stared at Jem and then at the paper in his hand. Jem offered it to her but she wouldn't take it. Jem had to read it to her: '*Count Zborowski died tragically while competing in the final day of the Prix d'Esmerelda's Birthday Cake motor race in Chitty Chitty*

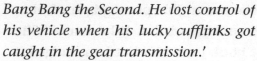

Bang Bang the Second. He lost control of his vehicle when his lucky cufflinks got caught in the gear transmission.'

'So you're saying . . . he dies today?'

'That's what it says here,' said Jem, 'but it's all right because we can save him. We can warn him not to wear his cufflinks or just tell him to take it a bit slower or . . .'

Lucy was quiet for a while, then she looked at her brother. 'We can't,' she said.

'Why not? Don't you want to save him?'

'Of course I want to save him. More than anything. But if we did, it would change the whole course of human history.'

'But how? It's not like the Count is anyone important . . .'

'Everyone is important. Everyone is connected.'

'But maybe if he'd lived he'd've done something really amazing, like found a cure for global warming or something.'

'Jem, we can't go round changing the course of history just because you think someone's got kind eyes.'

'I never said anything about his eyes.'

'It was a synecdoche. Look it up.' She left the tent.

Outside, Dad was cranking Chitty's engine.

'Come on, you Tootings!' he called. 'Let's show that newfangled Chitty what the Original and Best can do!'

On the other side of the picnic site Lucy saw the Count getting ready for the race, as Crackitt began loading everything into the biplane. As he pulled on his goggles, she saw the flash of his lucky cufflinks.

'We've got to tell him,' cried Jem, coming up behind her. 'We can't just stand by and watch him be killed.'

'You're right. So let's get going. Let's make sure we're miles ahead when it happens.'

She and Jem climbed into Chitty, where Mum and Red and Little Harry were already waiting.

'Lucy!' called the Count. 'Are you riding with me?'

Jem looked at her. He could see that she wanted to say yes. 'Lucy, you'll be killed,' he whispered.

'No, thank you, Count,' called Lucy.

'But I thought . . . Oh. You changed your mind.'

'That's right.'

'Girls do that a lot. See? I'm learning about girls. See you at the finish.'

'At the finish,' agreed Lucy, sniffing back a tear.

'Couldn't we at least tell him not to wear his cufflinks?' pleaded Jem.

But Dad had already slipped Chitty into reverse to get a better angle for joining the road. When Chitty was facing the right way, he slammed on her accelerator and she tore off down the highway.

At the first bend she came up behind the two cars that had rumbled past in the night. The sun shone so fiercely on her golden bodywork that the drivers in front were dazzled by their own rear-view mirrors and had to pull over to let her go. She bowled along the empty highway, her engine humming. So it was quite a surprise when, on the second bend, the shark-like silhouette of Chitty the Second sailed silently by.

'Ga gooo ga!' roared Chitty. The Count gave the Tootings a triumphant wave. And so did his passenger.

'Who's that riding with the Count?' said Mum.

'Oh no!' shrieked Jem. 'It's Lucy! She must have sneaked out of Chitty while Dad was reversing. Dad, you've got to catch up with them!'

'I realize that,' said Dad. 'This is a race, after all.'

'It's a lot more serious than that,' gasped Jem. He explained the terrible danger that Lucy was in.

But Chitty the Second was already disappearing into the distance.

'The booster engines. Remember the switch!' shouted Jem.

Dad tried to flip the switch which had made Chitty go so fast the day before, but now it wouldn't budge.

'What are we going to do?' sobbed Mum. 'Can we make her fly?'

'We never really found out how to do it except by driving off something high.'

'The falls. You could drive into the waterfall.'

By now Chitty the Second had all but disappeared into the distance. Dad saw that there was no alternative but to try to get Chitty to fly. At the next bend there was a slip road that led straight to the lake and the waterfall.

'Hold on, everyone,' called Dad, swinging the steering wheel to the left. But as quickly as he pulled it left, the wheel swung itself back to the right, keeping Chitty dead-centre in the middle of the road, heading straight after her rival.

'She. Won't. Budge,' wheezed Dad, still using all his strength on the wheel. 'We just have to drive after them.'

'Maybe,' said Mum, 'Chitty doesn't want to catch up. Maybe she's worried that if we race too hard, we'll make the Count go faster and crash.'

'But he's going to crash anyway. It's in the history books.'

'I think we have to do what we can,' said

Mum. 'And try to trust Chitty.'

On they powered, through the lanes and woods. By late afternoon they could see the towers and skyscrapers reaching into the sky. Then the air was filled with the sound of sirens. Blue lights flashed in the road ahead.

'It looks like there's been an accident,' said Dad.

No one else spoke.

But there hadn't been an accident. Two police cars were blocking the road. One policeman was talking to the Count. Another flagged down the Tootings.

'Sorry, lady, you can't go no further. Take a look at the sign.'

The sign said, 'New York Closed Due to Catastrophe.'

Mum jumped out of the car and hugged Lucy, who was standing at the side of the road. 'Oh, Lucy, how could you do such a thing?' she sobbed.

'I'm sorry, Mum, I just couldn't bear to see him drive off to his doom like that.'

The Count looked perfectly cheerful. 'Sorry about the delay,' he said. 'Anyone fancy a glass of champagne?'

'That would be illegal, sir,' said the policeman.

'So it would. You're quite right. Thanks for reminding me. Well, perhaps this obstruction is all for the best. No offence, Mrs Tooting, but although your daughter may be very informative she's not the ideal companion for a racing driver.'

'Really? Why?'

'She doesn't appreciate the technical details of motor racing. For instance, she kept telling me to slow down, which of course is exactly the wrong thing to do in a race. But which I had to do – what with her being a lady and asking politely. Also, she tried to get me to take off my lucky cufflinks. I did try to explain that without my lucky cufflinks, I wouldn't be lucky.'

'Oh dear. Perhaps she should finish the race in

Chitty then, instead of in Chitty the Second.'

'I hate to disappoint a lady,' said the Count, 'but I'm afraid that seems the only way.'

Red and Dad had meanwhile been asking the police about the roadblock.

'What kind of catastrophe is it anyway?' said Red.

'The catastrophic kind,' grunted the first policeman.

'We can't give any details for fear of creating a national panic,' said the second.

'Dad! Look out!' called Jem.

Chitty Chitty Bang Bang was somehow rolling backwards down the hill. All the Tootings, and Red, ran after her. One by one they managed to clamber on board, while Dad struggled to gain control of the wheel.

'Deer!' yelled Little Harry.

'Where?' said Mum. 'Oh no!'

A pair of beautiful young deer were standing in the middle of the road, not moving, just staring as though hypnotized by the sight of Chitty rumbling towards them. Any minute now she would hit them. Dad snatched at the wheel and Chitty bounced off the road and tumbled down an embankment. Seconds later, she flicked out her wings and swooped over the trees. She banked and turned back towards the line of the road, flying low over the heads of the police and the Count.

'I say!' shouted the Count. 'I hate to make a fuss, but isn't that cheating? This is supposed to be a road race not a sky race . . .'

Lucy waved down at him and watched him get smaller and smaller as they flew towards New York City. She felt in her heart that she would never see him again.

'Oh, if only he'd take off his cufflinks,' she said. 'But I don't think he will.'

*

The New York
catastrophe certainly did
seem to be catastrophic.
As they flew towards
the city, they saw
below them crowds of
people and columns of
cars pouring down the
highways, heading out of
town. Little Harry kept
leaning out and shouting,
'Hello, people!' Jem was
worried that he would
lose his balance and
plummet to his doom,
so he tied one end of
the prehistoric spider's
web around his wrist.
Chitty sailed elegantly
between the cliffs of glass
and concrete along Wall
Street, and came in to land
just outside the Bank of
America.

'Well, at least you're
safely home, Red,' said Mum.

'Home?' said Red. 'I don't want this to be home. I want to go back to El Dorado. We are going back to El Dorado, aren't we? That was the only place anyone ever played with me.'

'But what about your mother?' asked Mum. 'Won't she be missing you?'

'I ain't got no mother. Nor no father. And no grandmother now neither. Nearest thing I ever had to family was you. We're going back, aren't we? Say we are. All I do here is work. All I did there was play.'

'But this is your home town.'

'You sure?' said Red. 'It's normally a lot busier than this.'

Wall Street was completely deserted. Nothing was moving. Not a person. Not a car. They could hear water gushing from a fire hydrant a whole block away. The pavement glittered in the sunlight. They could hear birdsong – a flock of starlings tumbled past them just above their heads.

'Nice and peaceful,' said Dad.

'Peaceful?' said Red. 'Don't you ever notice anything? See that fire hydrant spouting water? Why isn't anyone doing anything about that? How did it get knocked over? See the way the pavement is shining? Can't you see why? Broken glass. Nearly every second-storey window here is broken.'

'Oh,' said Mum. 'Goodness. Maybe there was a tornado.'

'A tornado goes from ground to air,' said Lucy. 'It would have messed up the cars and mailboxes, not just the second-storey windows.'

'Some of the cars are messed up,' said Jem. 'Look at that one.'

At the side of the road were three cars: a beautiful cream-coloured Buick, a gorgeous navy-blue Pierce-Arrow and, in between these two, a twisted pile of scrap metal and shattered glass with some bent wheels sticking out of it.

'It looks like someone stood on it,' said Jem.

'Something that could crush a car like a biscuit tin,' said Lucy.

'And what,' said Red, 'was with the birds? What was their hurry? Like they were scared of something.'

There was a sound like a giant foot crushing a half-ton biscuit tin.

'That sound reminds me of something,' said Dad.

'Me too,' said Mum. 'What is it?'

The sound came again.

'I've never heard anything like that in my life,' said Red.

'But we have,' said Jem. 'I remember what it is now. I really think we should run.'

'Is this a new game?' asked Red.

'Dinosaur!' cried Little Harry and – right on cue – the head of a very hungry-looking Tyrannosaurus rex swung around the corner. Its vast yellow eyes scanned Wall Street, searching for food.

'Now this is what I call a game!' said Red. 'What're the rules?'

There was no answer. Everyone had run.

They ran towards the Stock Exchange. It looked like the perfect hiding place. The doors were too small for a tyrannosaur. There were hardly any windows to poke its head through. The walls were too thick to smash down. Perfect but for one thing: the doors were locked. Dad rattled at them but they wouldn't budge.

'We're trapped!' he gasped, turning round to see that the great beast was already trotting towards them, its huge tail balancing out its massive, swaying head.

'As a predator,' said Lucy, 'the tyrannosaurus is incredibly sensitive to movement. We need to stay out of its sight line and stay very, very still. Quick, behind here! Where's Red?'

Red came running towards them. At the top of the steps was a statue of a fat man in a top hat. The Tootings crouched down behind it, hardly daring to breathe.

Something tugged at Jem's wrist. He looked down and saw the special sticky spider's web leash he had tied to Little Harry's wrist. It was stretched tight.

'Oh no,' thought Jem, 'not again. Little Harry is out there somewhere. I'll pull him back in.'

He tugged at the web, trying to reel Little Harry in like a fish. Little Harry tugged back. Jem tugged harder but not too hard – he didn't want his younger brother to fall over. Little Harry came a bit nearer this time. He tugged again. Nearer again. It seemed to be working. Jem tugged one more time – a touch harder. Little Harry tugged back hard. Surprisingly hard. Shockingly hard. So hard that Jem was dragged out from behind the statue. Next thing he knew, he was being hauled down the steps. He tumbled and fell, but something – it couldn't be Little Harry, surely? – was dragging him across the pavement and now it was hoisting him into the air.

Jem screamed.

High above him he could see the drooling mouth of the tyrannosaurus like a hole in the sky. Below that were its fiddly claws . . . and in its claws was Little Harry. The leash that Jem had fastened to Little Harry's wrist was still there, tangled around one of the claws. When Jem had tugged on his end of the leash earlier, it wasn't Little Harry who had pulled back, it was the tyrannosaurus. And now

Jem was dangling from that leash, somewhere in the region of the dinosaur's scaly and surprisingly noisy belly.

That's a hungry dinosaur, thought Jem. In a minute it will be less hungry. Which will be thanks to me. But not in a good way.

He could have undone the leash. He could have dropped to the ground and run away.

But his brother was at the other end of the leash, so this is what Jem did. He gathered his courage and his strength. He took a handful of the leash and pulled himself upward. Hand over hand, he climbed up the leash to where his brother was trapped in the hellish claws of the infernal beast.

Gasping for breath, aching in every muscle, Jem hauled himself higher and higher until the moment came when he would have to touch the claw itself. He closed his eyes. He reached out. Cold and hard as stone it was, but moving, like a living statue. He reached over with his other hand and touched something warm . . . Little Harry.

'Dinosaur!' yelled Little Harry, helpfully.

'I did notice,' said Jem.

For someone who was trapped within the black claws and cold flesh of a dinosaur fist, Little Harry looked remarkably cheery.

'Dinosaur!' he reiterated.

194

'Honestly,' said Jem, 'I know.' The jaws lurched forward and sideways and back. Jem felt seasick. But he tried to keep thinking. There must be some way to get Little Harry down.

The great jaws closed up, teeth grinding, breath steaming. The massive eyes swivelled and descended. The dinosaur was staring at Little Harry.

'Dinosaur!'

An oily rumble came from somewhere deep within the dark well of its throat.

'Shhh, Harry.'

'Dinosaur!'

The same rumble from the same dark well.

'Dinosaur!'

There it was again.

Little Harry, thought Jem, and the dinosaur . . . They're talking to each other.

'Dinosaur!'

Rumble!

'Dinosaur!'

Rumble!

'Little Harry,' said Jem, 'do you know this dinosaur?'

'My dinosaur! My egg!'

'You do know him, don't you? Let me guess.' It had suddenly all become very clear to Jem. 'You stole this egg from the Cretaceous period, when it was still an egg. You carried it round with you for days in that little red bag. You hatched the dinosaur from an egg, didn't you, Harry? And then somehow left the baby dinosaur behind in New York when we went to El Dorado.'

'Egg . . . all gone,' sighed Little Harry.

'You hatched it from an egg,' said Jem, 'and now it thinks that you're its mother!'

'Mummy!' yelled Little Harry.

From far away Jem could hear his own mother howl, 'Harrrrrryyyy!!!'

But much nearer and much louder was the cheerful gurgle in the tyrannosaur's throat. A gurgle that clearly meant 'Mummy yourself' in Tyrannosaurese.

'Oh,' said Jem, 'he's just a baby! A baby who thinks you're his mummy. A baby who'll follow his mummy wherever she goes.'

Just at that moment the dinosaur jerked its head away from them, and groaned, as though it had been slapped. When it tried to turn back, it winced

and groaned again, screwing up its eyes. Someone was flashing a light into them.

It was Red. Far below them, on the pavement of Wall Street, Red was holding something above his head, something that sent a brilliant light straight into the eyes of the dinosaur.

'Red!' said Mum. 'Where on earth did you get that?'

'The main square in El Dorado,' said Red. The object in his hand was the Diamond As Big As Your Head.

'You stole the Diamond As Big As Your Head!' gasped Mum.

'I didn't steal it. I was going to give it to you. As a present. For saving my life. It's lucky I did too. Because this is going to save your kids' lives.'

He flashed it one more time. The dinosaur growled and tried to shade its eye with its tiny claw. As it did so, its claw opened and Jem and Little Harry fell.

'Jem! Harry!' yelled Mum and Dad as their sons whistled downward past the scales and muscles of the tyrannosaur.

But just before they were smashed to pieces on the pavement, they were whipped back into the air again, then down again, and up again, and down again. They were still attached to the length

198

of Cretaceous spider's web. One end was wrapped around the tyrannosaur's claw and the other around their bodies. They had completed history's only Tyrannosaurus Bungee Jump.

'OK, Little Harry,' said Jem as they stopped bouncing and finally got their feet on the ground. 'We have to get to Chitty. Go on. Go.'

'Do walkings?'

'Yes, do walkings.'

Little Harry toddled off across Wall Street, with the gigantic tyrannosaur obediently following behind, on the end of the leash.

'Into the car, Little Harry! Into the car!' said Jem. Then he called, 'Mum! Dad! Everyone! To Chitty!'

Lucy was the first to realize what had happened. She explained everything. 'It's called "imprinting",' she said. 'When a bird or a reptile hatches from its egg, the first thing it sees, it calls Mummy. This dinosaur thinks Little Harry is its mummy. Jem has attached it to Little Harry using his leash. All we have to do is pop Little Harry in Chitty, drive Chitty back to the Cretaceous period, towing the tyrannosaur after us, and turn it loose. Easy.'

'Couldn't be easier,' said Dad.

'Except,' said Red, 'for the plane.'

'What plane?'

'The plane with all the guns and bombs and stuff.'

A small red biplane, engine whining like a wasp, guns splattering the pavement with bullets, was heading down Wall Street straight for the dinosaur, which meant it was also heading straight for Chitty, and Jem and Little Harry.

'The rest of you run,' shouted Red. 'I'll try to use the diamond to dazzle the pilot.'

The others ran and leaped into Chitty while Red angled the diamond to catch the sun.

The plane kept coming.

The bullets kept firing. Red lifted the diamond higher and leaned back as far as he could. Suddenly the firing stopped.

Jem looked up to wave a thank-you to the pilot. Then he saw why the firing had stopped. It wasn't Red's doing at all. The pilot had stopped firing because he was going to do something much, much worse. As the plane turned overhead, flying so low that Jem could easily see its struts and wheels, the pilot leaned out and dropped a small black object over the side.

'Bomb!' smiled Little Harry.

'Bomb!' shrieked Jem.

'Bomb!' yelled Mum.

'Ga gooo ga!' (That was Chitty.)

'Gurgle!' said the tyrannosaur, which – as we know – translates roughly as 'MUM!', by which he meant Little Harry. Little Harry was pointing up at the bomb as it fell. The tyrannosaur clearly took this as an order and, with an almighty swish of its tail, whacked the bomb back into the air, as if it had been a baseball and its tail a baseball bat.

The bomb exploded with a puff of harmless smoke just above Federal Hall. It wasn't much of a bomb really.

'Quick! To Chitty!' yelled Jem.

Little Harry climbed into the back seat, while Mum cranked her up and Dad started the engine. He drove slowly forward, giving Mum the chance to jump in. The dinosaur – still on the end of its leash, still thinking that Little Harry was its mummy – trotted along behind. Anyone who was looking out of a window that day would have seen a gold-plated vintage car carrying a family from the future towing an obedient Tyrannosaurus rex by a lead.

'What's that noise?' said Jem. 'It sounds like rain but I don't feel anything.'

No sooner had he said this than he *did* feel something. A long, thin strip of paper landed on his head. Another landed on Mum's, another on the windscreen. Strips of paper were flying everywhere.

'This is ticker tape,' said Lucy. 'It's what they used for information before computers . . .'

A storm of ticker tape was blowing all around them.

'Where's it coming from?'

'Look! Up there!' Every window higher than the second floor was packed with faces. When the dinosaur started its rampage on Wall Street, the people who had been out and about had fled to the subway or jumped into their cars. But everyone who was inside a building had simply run upstairs to get a better view. They guessed – rightly – that the dinosaur would not be able to manage the elevators and that they would be quite safe and thoroughly entertained if they stayed at the windows. They had seen the whole drama. They had gasped in horror when the creature had picked up the baby; cheered encouragement when Jem had climbed up to rescue him; howled in despair when the plane dropped its bomb; and cheered again when the dinosaur had batted away the bomb with its tail.

'A gold-plated car towing a tame dinosaur!' said one man. 'I could wait a week and not see anything as surprising as this!'

'That kid who saved the baby!' said one woman. 'Do I know him from somewhere?'

'Sure you do. He's Jem Diamonds,' said her friend, 'the notorious getaway driver. He's the one who outdrove the whole police department before getting away in a boat. He's a notorious criminal.'

'But also a hero. The way he rescued that baby. Made me wanna swoon! You got any more of that ticker tape?'

'This is a ticker-tape parade!' said Dad. 'They're giving us a ticker-tape parade – one of the highest honours New York can bestow . . .'

'What are they shouting?'

'It sounds like "Jem, Jem, Jem, Jem",' said Lucy. 'Why would they be shouting "Jem"?'

'They can't be,' said Jem. 'You must have misheard them.' But all the same he stood up and waved. An almighty cheer rang up and down Wall Street.

'At the corner of Broadway,' said Mum, 'we'll turn left into the Cretaceous period. Hold on to your hats, everybody . . .'

So at the corner of Broadway, Chitty Chitty Bang Bang made a neat left turn and neither she nor the dinosaur was ever seen in New York again.

On the upper storeys of the Stock Exchange, the cheering crowds didn't notice the little red-headed boy running after the car, shouting, 'Stop! Stop! Wait for me!'

12

When you turn left out of Wall Street on to Broadway, the first thing you see is Trinity Church. If you are the Tootings, the next thing you see is a wide water meadow where deer go bouncing from tussock to tussock. Drive straight across that meadow and quite quickly you come to the Ice Age (you'll know that by the mammoths and sabre-tooth tigers). If you turn left there, you'll come to a thick forest where big shaggy mammals go shambling by. Keep going and you'll soon find the trees get taller and denser. After that you should see a primeval swamp with brontosauruses lolloping around in it.

That's where they stopped.

All was silent, save for the constant whirr of giant dragonfly wings and the gurgling of the tyrannosaurus.

Carefully Jem undid the leash around Little Harry's wrist. 'Say goodbye, Little Harry,' he whispered.

'Goodbye, Little Harry,' said Little Harry, trying to climb out of the car. Clearly he was thinking of staying in the Cretaceous period with his dinosaur.

'No, say goodbye to the dinosaur.'

Little Harry waved to the tyrannosaur. The tyrannosaur put its head to one side. It seemed to know that they were about to abandon it.

'All set?' said Dad.

'Couldn't we just wait a minute?' said Mum. 'The poor thing looks a bit lost.'

Even as she said this, the tyrannosaur's nostrils twitched. It turned its head. It had seen the lolloping great brontosauruses and it had thought to itself – lunch. Its tail swung over their heads. The ground shook. It thundered towards the water's edge. The brontosauruses turned slowly and saw it coming. They didn't move. They had seen the tyrannosaur but their brains could only do one thing at a time. At the moment they were telling their jaws to chew leaves. If there was time a bit later, their brains might think *Emergency: better run*, but it would take that message so long to travel the hundred feet to their legs that really they might just as well concentrate on chewing.

The tyrannosaur got nearer and nearer.

'This is going to be really gory!' said Lucy. 'There's going to be blood and destruction everywhere. Can we stay and watch?'

'I really think,' said Dad, 'that we should get out of here in case we end up as dessert.'

He slammed Chitty into reverse, giving her a good run-up, and then zoomed towards the swamp, while tugging on the Chronojuster. Before they even reached it, the swamp was a frozen waste. By the time they had gone a mile across that, it was a wide prairie . . .

'Dinosaur!' sobbed Little Harry.

'He'll be all right,' said Lucy, slipping an arm around her brother. 'Just think about his big claws and surprisingly useful tail. He's a happy little dinosaur – he'll be back there now, killing and eating all kinds of other dinosaurs and having a great time . . .' But thinking about the abandoned dinosaur made her suddenly remember someone else. 'Hey,' she said, 'what happened to Red?'

Millions of years in the future, Red had done his best to catch up with Chitty, but by the time he got to Broadway, she had vanished. He looked around. There was still not a soul on the streets. Alone in the middle of a vast, deserted city, hundreds of years away from the happiest time of his life, he felt lonelier than anyone has ever felt in the whole history of this world. So it's no surprise that when, finally, someone did appear on the street, he almost ran over to them. They were a man and a woman. Almost like a mum and a dad. They seemed to be looking for something. Maybe they were even looking for a little boy. When he got closer, he recognized them. It was Lenny Manmountain and Bella Sposa. Bella had got rid of her wedding outfit and was now dressed all in red, wearing red sunglasses and with red-painted fingernails. Had the Tootings been there, they might have thought that she looked uncannily like Nanny. The very Nanny who, strangely unaged, was currently living in their house along with Tiny Jack.

Even though they had recently kidnapped his friends, tied them up and left them in a barn, he was still pleased to see their familiar faces.

'Hi,' said Red. 'Remember me?'

'Of course I remember you,' smiled Nanny. 'The boy with the lovely red hair.'

'You recently kidnapped my friends, tied them up and left them in a barn.'

'So we did,' purred Nanny. 'We apologize for any inconvenience we may have caused. Where are those friends now?'

'Well,' said Red. 'They sort of dumped me, I guess.'

'Dumped you?' said Nanny. 'What a pity. In that case, why not make the best of the situation and join us instead? We believe in making the best of a situation, don't we, Lenny?'

'We do,' said Manmountain. 'For instance, in the current situation, people see a big, mean lizard and run away. Many times in doing so they drop their wallet, or their cash, or even their shopping, which may contain diamond bracelets for all I know. So we pick them up before people get wise to the fact that the dinosaur is gone.'

'And if you ask me,' said Nanny, 'it is gone before it even came. Maybe it is not a real dinosaur at all, but just a hysterical illusion. The loot, however, is real and we are grateful for your help in raking it in – as we are more than somewhat short of money at the present – thanks to this big lummox.' She jerked her thumb at Manmountain. 'Promised me he was going to rob all the gold in the Federal Gold Reserve just for me! Said he was going to make us rich. And now look at us, picking up nickels and dimes from wallets in the street. A girl has to get used to disappointment in this life.'

Red looked up and down the deserted Broadway. He thought how happy he had been with the Tootings and Chitty. How hard life had been before

209

they came. How they had left without even saying goodbye, and forgotten all about him. Abandoned him in an empty city with no friend and no family. No one to play with. 'So,' he said, 'you like gold?'

'Gold, diamonds, the secret of eternal youth – my tastes are simple,' said Nanny. 'Give me gold, and diamonds, and I am yours to command.'

'Would you really?' asked Red. 'Be mine to command? Just for diamonds?'

'To be honest, it would depend on the quantity and also the size of the diamonds.'

'What if it was a single diamond, but one as big as your head?'

Nanny stared. Red was holding up the Diamond As Big As Your Head.

'Kid,' she said, 'I'm all yours. Just hand that over.'

'I will if you play with me?'

'What?'

'I like to play games. And I've got no one to play with. If I give you the diamond will you play with me?'

'Why, sure we will play with you. We will play all kinds of games. Did you ever play bank robbers? Or blackmailers? Hijackers? We can play all these games together, can't we, Lenny?'

'Sure we can, kid. What's your name?'

'He already tells you his name. His name is Red.'

'Too hard. Can we call him Jack?'

'We are already confused on account of the number of Jacks we know. For instance, Jack the Dice, Jack the Hat, Hasty Jack, Two-Face Jack, Three-Face Jack, Halloween Jack . . .'

'But this Jack is different. He has a Diamond As Big As Your Head and also red hair. How can we confuse him with waste-of-time people such as those you mention? I votes we name him Tiny Jack.'

'Tiny Jack,' said Red. 'I like that. Let's play bank robbers . . .'

Hundreds of years in the past, the Tootings were tootling through medieval Mexico on their way home from the Cretaceous period. They paused for a while to watch the Aztecs put the finishing touch to a giant pyramid. The Aztec pyramid rose up, then brambles and cacti grew all over it in the time that it took Chitty to slip into the air.

They flew across the Atlantic, which was mostly covered in ice, then not very covered in ice, then almost all covered in ice again. Soon Chitty was dipping towards the White Cliffs of Dover, bumping over the turf towards the A20. It was good to be breathing the fresh sea air (which was completely free of pterodactyls or bullets) and to look down on the bright blue bay (which contained neither piranhas nor alligators). Soon they had landed on the dear familiar road with its helpful road signs, so different from the twisting and mysterious forest pathways of Amazonia. When passers-by tooted or waved, they all waved back. Chitty always made people stop and stare. More so than ever, now that she was covered in gold.

They stopped for petrol. It was the very service station they had stopped at on the day Jem realized that the little model plane he'd been given by the man in the scrapyard was Chitty's mascot: the magical Zborowski Lightning.

'We were just about here,' said Jem, looking around nervously, 'last time Tiny Jack tried to kill us.'

They shuddered. They had all forgotten who was waiting for them in Zborowski Terrace.

'Of course! We can't go home!' cried Jem. 'Tiny Jack is waiting for us. We have to go back to 1966 and get the Potts to help us.'

'Why should we let Tiny Jack scare us out of our own home?' said Mum.

'Because,' explained Lucy, 'he's very scary.'

'But we are the Tooting family. We've faced dinosaurs and gangsters and anacondas. We're not scared of Tiny Jack. Or Tiny Anything Else. We can defeat Tiny Jack on our own. We don't need the Potts to help us. Time to go home.'

13

It seemed no time at all before they had parked Chitty outside the house in the middle of Zborowski Terrace. They got out and lined up. They all held hands, ready to face whatever danger lay inside. They might have hesitated. They might have changed their minds. But before they had the chance, the front door opened itself and the kettle switched itself on.

'I'd forgotten all about the automatic welcome!' said Mum. 'How lovely.'

They went inside.

Everything looked just how they had left it the day they set out on holiday. There on the dining table were the sunglasses Dad had forgotten. Leaning against the wall was Jem's surfboard – which they'd decided was too big to bring. There was a pile of newspapers ready for recycling. It was as though they had only just gone.

There was no sign of Tiny Jack. Or Nanny. Or anyone else.

'Are we sure they're not hiding upstairs?' said Jem.

'I'll go and see,' said Mum.

'Careful!'

'I can wrestle anacondas. I'm not scared of a nanny.'

There was nothing upstairs but their own dear bedrooms. The walls of the landing were covered with framed family photographs: pictures of Lucy holding Little Harry, of Mum and Dad getting married, of Jem in his first school uniform. Of everyone on the beach in Dorset.

'We used to think it was exciting going to Dorset,' said Dad, who had come upstairs now that he knew it was safe. 'But now that we've been to El Dorado . . .'

'It *was* exciting. It was lovely, too. Oh look!' said Mum, pointing at another photo. 'That was the day you caught the fish!'

'It's nice to be home,' said Dad.

'It's wonderful to be home.'

'Tea's ready!' called Jem. 'I'm going to go and get some milk and biscuits from Mr Ainsworth's shop.'

Jem felt strangely happy walking round to Mr Ainsworth's. He pushed his hands deep into his pockets, felt the sun on his face and enjoyed the comfortable feeling of knowing exactly where he was going and what he was doing, without worrying about pumas or gangsters.

A bell rang at the door of the shop as he strolled in. Mr Ainsworth came through from the back and said, 'Hello, Jem.'

'Hi, Mr Ainsworth,' replied Jem, thinking how nice it was when people knew your name. He put the milk on the counter along with the packet of ginger biscuits he'd picked out.

'Not seen you for a while. You want to start delivering the papers again?'

'Yes, I suppose so,' said Jem, taking a paper.

'Been somewhere nice?'

'Just here and there.'

'Home now, though. Best to be home for Christmas.'

'Christmas?' gasped Jem.

'Don't say you've forgotten it's Christmas!?' laughed Mr Ainsworth.

Jem grabbed the milk, the paper and the biscuits and hurried home. He saw them now – the signs of Christmas all the way up Zborowski Terrace. On the lawn of number three stood a highly decorative plastic sleigh and six almost full-size plastic reindeer with lit-up antlers. A twinkly electric shooting star was parked above the door of number seven. On the roof of number nine, a giant inflatable Santa sat hunched over the chimney pot.

'Dad!' he shouted as he burst through the front door. 'It's Christmas . . .'

'Christmas?' said Dad. 'Did you hear that, everyone? It's Christmas. Come on, let's get the decorations up.'

The Tooting family Christmas tree was a real tree – a blue spruce – growing in a pot outside on the patio. Every year they brought it in and every year Dad played the game of pretending it was too big to bring inside the house. It never quite was, but this year it was close. The top of the tree just touched the ceiling when Jem and Dad moved it into its traditional position in front of the French windows. The Tooting family decorations were kept in a big box behind the water tank in the loft. Dad said that Lucy could climb up and get them since she liked dark, damp spider's-webby places so much. Lucy climbed up and sat for a while behind the water tank, thinking about how quickly even the most exciting day turns into yesterday, then she brought the box of decorations down to the living room. She and Dad and Jem began to sort them. Mum stood staring out of the window.

The decorations had been collected over many years. In a way, they were like a little history of the Tooting family. Here was the cardboard and glitter angel that Lucy had made at playgroup. Here was the robin that was made from Little Harry's handprint.

'And look,' said Lucy. 'Here's the crib that Jem made as a present to us all. Remember? The crib with five kings and no baby Jesus. Because he had silver plasticine for the crowns and forgot about Jesus completely.'

'And here's the drawing Lucy did,' said Jem, 'of King Herod killing the innocent babies. And when Mum said it wasn't Christmassy she said, "Well, it must have been round Christmas time."'

'Oh yes,' said Dad, 'she really loved drawing pictures of severed limbs. And do you know what this is . . . ?'

'Yes, Dad, you tell us every year.'

He was holding up a pair of delicate, sparkly little angels. 'These,' he said, 'were the first decorations we ever bought. We didn't even have a tree. We just had these two angels – one each.'

He sneaked up behind Mum and quietly hung

the angels, one on each of her ears. She turned around, ready to tick him off, but then she saw the decorations the children had put up. Jem had already set the Advent candles on the table. Lucy had already strung red ribbons from the light fittings.

'Christmas,' sighed Mum. 'Christmas in our own house. Where else would we want it to be? Bring me the ladder, I'll put the angel on top of the tree.'

'You know,' said Dad, as he helped Mum down from the ladder. 'We went to some amazing places and met some amazing people, but no one was as amazing as you are, and nowhere is as wonderful as this.'

Mum leaned down and kissed him on the nose. Which was bad enough. But then he kissed her on the lips.

'OK, you've just ruined Christmas,' said Lucy. 'I'm going to my room. Call me in the New Year.'

The moment she walked back into her room,

though, Lucy's heart skipped a beat. Here were her books, her models, her drawings, her notebooks. Here were all the pieces of Lucy that Lucy had forgotten about. Plus there was a door. It had been a long time since Lucy had been able to close the door and loll about in a room of her own, just thinking and listening to the house stretch and rumble around her. She turned on her computer, her mind on all the Facebook updates that would be waiting for her – all the bits of news and gossip, everything that had happened while she was away. How lovely it was going to be to catch up with all that. How strange it was to have had so many adventures but be back in their own house, with hardly any time gone.

She thought about how nearly they had changed the whole course of human history by accidentally taking a dinosaur to New York. But the dinosaur did change the course of the race. The race in which the Count was killed. Maybe he didn't die after all? She turned on her computer. All she had to do was look him up on Wikipedia, then she'd know his final fate. What if it was something worse? What if he was still alive? While the computer booted up, she knelt up on her bed and looked out of the window. Snow was falling through the street lights.

That's strange, thought Lucy. I didn't notice

that it was snowing. She pressed her face against the window to get a better view. 'Oh!' she said. 'It's not real snow at all.' Moving down Zborowski Terrace was a machine like a kind of grit-spreader – but it wasn't spreading grit. It was spreading snow. A thick carpet of perfect white snow. Moving along that carpet, just behind the snow-spreader, was a beautiful, enchanting sight. A sleigh – a real sleigh – pulled by a dozen very real reindeer. In the driver's seat was a woman dressed like the Snow Queen, and next to her was someone dressed as an elf. Children came running out of all the houses to get a closer look.

'Mum! Dad!' shouted Lucy. 'Look out of the window.'

'What?'

'Look. Just look.'

Lucy settled down at her desk and as her computer took itself online, she listened to the excited voices discussing whether they really were real reindeer, and how many there were, and what were they doing there and . . . were those other children getting a ride on it?

She listened as the front door opened and Mum led Little Harry out into the street. She watched as Mum carried Little Harry right up to the sleigh.

*

The Snow Queen lady smiled from under her fur-trimmed hood and asked Mum if Little Harry would like to sit up alongside her.

'He's just a bit nervous,' said Mum. 'Maybe I could get up there with him.'

'I'm afraid we have a height limit,' shrugged the lady. 'It's a health and safety thing.'

'I'll go with him,' said Jem. 'Unless I'm too tall too.'

'No, you're just right. Is it all right with Mum? If big brother looks after Little Harry?'

'I think so,' said Mum.

So Jem boosted Little Harry up on to the beautiful sleigh.

'Well, isn't this exciting?' said the lady with the hood. She raised her whip and cracked it over the backs of the reindeer. The reindeer leaped in their harnesses and galloped off down the street.

'Doesn't that look incredibly dangerous?' said Dad, who had come out to see what was happening.

'Nothing wrong with a bit of incredible danger,' said Mum.

'But isn't it a bit odd?' said Dad.

The neighbours were leading their children back indoors. The children tugged at them, wanting to follow the sleigh. Lucy came out into the artificial snow.

'There's something very strange happening,' she said. 'According to Facebook it's the fifteenth of June.'

'There's something wrong with your computer,' said Mum. 'Everyone knows that Christmas is the twenty-fifth of December.'

'That's what I thought. Then I looked at the newspaper Jem bought earlier. That says the fifteenth of June too.'

Just then, Mr Ainsworth from the shop went by on his bicycle. 'Happy Christmas!' he called.

'Happy Christmas!' said Mum. 'See, Lucy? Of course it's Christmas. Little Harry and Jem just went for a ride on Santa's sleigh.'

'Mr Ainsworth,' said Lucy, 'how many shopping days to go to Christmas Day?'

Without a second's hesitation and with a merry chuckle in his voice, Mr Ainsworth replied, 'Just a hundred and sixty-four shopping days to go.'

'A hundred and sixty-four? Isn't that quite a lot? Doesn't that mean it's . . .'

'June the fifteenth,' said Lucy. 'It's not Christmas at all.'

'It didn't used to be Christmas,' agreed Mr Ainsworth, stopping his bicycle. 'But ever since Tiny Jack came to live here, there's no such thing as Not Christmas. He wants it to be Christmas every day. Always Christmas, that's his motto. Always Christmas and never winter.'

'Did you just say,' said Dad, looking down the street to where the sleigh was careering round the corner and out of sight, 'did you just say "Tiny Jack"?'

'The very same. Why, he's the living spirit of Christmas. Well. Must go. Ho ho ho.'

Mr Ainsworth pedalled off.

'To Chitty!' shouted Dad. 'We have to follow that sleigh.'

The sleigh bounced down Zborowski Terrace and on to the main road. Cars pulled over to let it past. Drivers leaned out to take photographs with their phones. They didn't hear Jem shouting, 'Call the police! Call my mum!'

Soon the sleigh was at a slip road to the motorway, where it stopped. Jem grabbed Little Harry and tried to jump free, but with amazing dexterity, the woman in the cloak cracked her whip, and it wound itself around Jem's feet. Holding him by the shoulder, she pulled Santa's sack from the back of the sleigh, and pushed it over Jem's head, then stuffed Little Harry in after him.

Plunged into darkness, the two boys could not

see what the drivers could see: a large helicopter made of Lego dropping out of the sky towards them, and the woman whipping off her hood to reveal a mass of gorgeous red hair. It was Nanny.

Seconds later, a winch descended from the helicopter. Nanny grabbed it and, with the two boys in a bag over her shoulder, she was hauled skywards. Once she was aboard the helicopter, it soared off over the Downs towards Dover.

Inside the sack, Jem and Little Harry could hear Nanny laughing. 'Look behind us, Tiny Jack,' she trilled. 'Somebody wants to play . . .'

Chitty Chitty Bang Bang flew through the night, hard on the tail of the chopper. Into and out of the moonlit clouds, over the White Cliffs of Dover and out to sea, skimming the waves. Until up ahead they saw what looked like a small town rising out of the waves.

'Château Bateau!' cried Lucy. 'Look! They're landing on the main deck.'

'Tiny Jack's evil lair. We can't land there – he'll feed us to the piranhas.'

'I'd like to see him try,' snapped Mum. She grabbed the steering wheel and brought Chitty skimming in to land between two great chunks of standing stone.

224

'Crikey,' said Lucy, as she stepped on to the deck. 'Look! He's stolen Stonehenge.'

'Yes, that was a bit naughty,' came a voice from behind them.

Nanny.

At the same moment they were all struck by how strangely like Bella Sposa she looked. But how was that possible?

'How nice of you to bring the car,' she purred, 'and to polish her bodywork so brightly. Why, she almost looks as if she's made of gold. Tiny Jack will be pleased. He does love gold. He's tucked up safe in bed just now, the little darling. I'll wake him. I can't wait to see his face. This is quite the nicest thank-you present ever. You really shouldn't have.'

'Thank you for what?' snapped Dad.

'Thank you for giving you back your children,' smiled Nanny.

She pointed to the Santa's sack, which was dangling from a wire, hanging over the piranha pool. The water in the pool boiled with hungry fish.

'I have to admit that in the past we have thought of trying to steal Chitty from you, but really you're all so clever, we found we couldn't do it. And besides, it's so much nicer to get things as a present, don't you think? Tiny Jack loves it when people just give me things. For instance, you could give us Chitty Chitty Bang Bang. And we could give you Little Harry and Jem.'

The Tootings stepped away from Chitty. Nanny pressed a button on a small remote she took from her pocket, and the water drained from the piranha pool, leaving the fish gasping and drowning. 'Looks like it's fish for tea again tonight,' she sighed. When the fish had stopped flopping, she let Little Harry and Jem out of the sack.

'Mummy!' yelled Little Harry, running back to Mum.

'That's right,' said Mum. 'Mummy is here.'

'And so, finally, is Tiny Jack,' smiled Nanny.

A little figure had appeared at Nanny's side. The Tootings stared. At last they were face to face with their Nemesis, their evil arch-enemy. All the Tootings gasped.

'But Tiny Jack,' stammered Dad, 'you're Red. Our little friend Red. The boy we . . .'

'The boy,' snarled Tiny Jack, 'that you abandoned in New York all those years ago.'

'Don't feel too bad about it,' smiled Nanny. 'After all, you did leave him with a diamond as big as your head and two hardened criminals to take care of him. Really a very good start in life.'

'You look well on it,' said Mum. 'You haven't changed a bit.' It was true that Tiny Jack seemed not to have grown an inch. He still had a mop of thick curly red hair, even though he must be a hundred and twenty years old by now. 'What's your secret?'

'Tiny Jack is fabulously wealthy,' said Nanny. 'Money can buy you anything, even youth.'

When Jem looked closer though, he could see that Tiny Jack had changed really. His eyes were dull and mean and weary. His fingernails were bitten to the quick. His hands were old.

'You all forgot about me. And all I wanted was to play a few games.'

'He just wants to play,' sighed Nanny. 'He really does love to play.'

'Dear Red . . .' said Mum.

'It's Tiny Jack,' said Tiny Jack. 'Not Red.'

'We didn't just leave you behind,' said Lucy. 'We would have liked to take you with us. But we thought if we did, that would change the course of history. We were always trying not to change history. We even let poor Count Louis drive to his doom in the end.'

'History,' sneered Tiny Jack. 'I OWN history.' He pointed to Stonehenge and to the Sphinx and all the other great treasures he had stolen.

'We could play a game now,' said Dad. 'We've got Travel Scrabble in the car.'

'Too late!' roared Tiny Jack. 'Soon I will play a different kind of game. A game called Destruction. Cities will be my pieces. Death will be my dice.'

'What about hide-and-seek?' said Mum.

'Take them away!' roared Tiny Jack. 'Take them for one last ride in Chitty Chitty Bang Bang. One last ride in my car.'

When Nanny cranked the engine and climbed into the driver's seat, a great hope arose in Jem's heart. Even as the Tootings got in behind her, he thought that Chitty wouldn't start: not for her; only for them.

Chitty started first time. Nanny drove her straight to the edge of the cliff and over it.

Of course! It was a trap! Chitty would surely crash into the sea and rid the world once and for all of that terrible supervillain and his nanny.

But Chitty floated lazily over the sea on her gorgeous wings.

Soon they were each lost in their individual memories of their Chitty adventures. Lucy thought about her last sight of the Count; Jem of the Golden City; Mum and Dad of the breathless nights of partying in Manhattan. Dinosaurs, thought Little

Harry. Each of them was so lost in their daydreams, they were all surprised to find that Nanny had parked on a busy London street.

'Everyone out,' she said.

Obediently they stepped out on to the pavement while she settled once more into the driver's seat.

'You'll never get away with this,' said Dad.

'Chitty won't let you,' said Mum. 'She likes us. She'll never let you take her away.'

'I'm the only one who understands her,' said Jem. 'We're not going to let you keep her. We'll get her back somehow.'

'Somehow I don't think so,' said Nanny. 'I've come up with a simple but brilliant way to stop you stealing her back.' She slipped the handbrake and readied the clutch.

'Oh really?' sneered Jem defiantly.

'Oh really, really, really, really, really,' smiled Nanny, before adding, 'Really.'

She drove off. A few minutes later they saw a small shape with powerful headlamps soaring high over the rooftops.

It was only when she had gone that they realized that the people around them looked different from the normal London crowd. They were mostly men and nearly all of them were wearing hats. Mostly woollen hats with matching scarfs. Some of them were wearing rosettes and carrying wooden rattles.

'Football!' shouted Little Harry.

'He's right,' said Jem. 'She's put us down outside a football match.'

'Oh!' said Dad, looking up at the white domed building across the road. 'That's the old Wembley Stadium. She might have left us a bit nearer home.'

'You mean,' said Lucy, 'the old Wembley Stadium with its iconic two towers built in 1923 and described by Pelé as the Cathedral of Football . . .'

'That's right,' said Dad, 'dear old Wembley.'

'The Wembley Stadium that was demolished in 2003?'

'Ah,' said Dad.

'Oh,' said Jem. 'Nanny hasn't just left us in London. She's left us in the past.'

'But how long in the past?'

Dad stopped a passing family – a mum, a dad and two children – and asked them who was playing.

'Who's playing?' said the father, a distinguished-looking man in a Navy uniform.

'Who's playing?' laughed the little boy.

'Why, England of course!' said the girl.

'England and Germany,' said the mother.

Jem was staring at this family. He seemed to have seen them somewhere before.

'It's the World Cup Final,' said the man in the Navy uniform. 'And after that, fish and chips. Good afternoon.' He marched briskly towards the turnstiles, taking his family with him.

'England in the World Cup Final!' said Dad.

'How unbelievably exciting,' said Mum, squeezing his hand.

'The Potts!' said Jem. 'That's who they were. The man in the Navy uniform was Commander Pott, and the children were Jeremy and Jemima. We searched the Amazon for them and now we've found them in north London.'

'How lovely!' said Mum. 'We'll have so much to talk to them about.'

'Doesn't anyone understand what's happening here?' spluttered Lucy. 'When was the last time England were in a World Cup Final?'

'1966 of course,' said Dad. 'Everyone knows that.'

'So where are we now?'

'We are in 19 . . . Oh,' said Dad.

'Exactly. Nanny and Tiny Jack are worried that we'll try to get Chitty back. So they've solved that problem by dumping us in the past.'

'Perfect,' said Jem.

'How is that perfect?' said Lucy, 'We're in London thirty years before we were even born. With no way of getting back to our own time and now an evil supervillain and his nanny have got the means to travel back and forth in time doing whatever evil thing they please.'

'We're in the same time and the same city as the Potts. If we join forces with them we know we can defeat Tiny Jack once and for all. And maybe even get Chitty back for good.'

'You're so right,' said Mum. 'Quick, everyone! After them!'